"A 1990's coming-of-age story with special appeal."
—*The San Diego Union*

"Ferris's uniquely individual characters are drawn with winning sympathy; their dialogue sparkles with wisdom and humor."
—*Kirkus Reviews*

"Thought-provoking ideas about commitment, dependence, and self-discovery."
—*Publishers Weekly*

AN ALA BEST BOOK FOR YOUNG ADULTS

ACROSS THE GRAIN

Other books by Jean Ferris

AMEN, MOSES GARDENIA

THE STAINLESS STEEL RULE

INVINCIBLE SUMMER

LOOKING FOR HOME

RELATIVE STRANGERS

Across the Grain

JEAN FERRIS

aerial fiction Farrar Straus Giroux

Library of Congress catalog card number: 90-55472
Distributed in Canada by Douglas & McIntyre Ltd.
Printed in the United States of America
First edition, 1990
Aerial edition, 1993
12 11 10 9 8 7 6 5 4 3

This book was made possible, in part, by a grant co-sponsored by Judy Blume and the Society of Children's Book Writers.

FOR NANCY ACKER

ACROSS THE GRAIN

1

The same gray sliver of soap that had been there the day before lay in the shower's soap dish. That meant there wouldn't be any orange juice either, Will thought as he tried to coax some lather out of the exhausted scrap.

Yesterday had been Paige's turn to go to the market. At least the towels were clean. Yesterday had been his turn to do the laundry.

How come, when he went to school all day and then straight to his job at Pizza on Wheels, studying while he waited for orders to come in, he could still get his chores done? Why, when all Paige did was teach three aerobic classes a day, could she never find time to do hers? Why, when that was the way she'd always been, did he still expect something different from his sister?

On the way back to his room, he stuck his head through the half-open door to the other bedroom. Paige lay face down, arms outflung, on top of her rumpled bed—what she called her Life-Support System since, somewhere in its folds and furrows, it usually contained the telephone, several changes of clothing, some kind of food, and the latest copy of *Cosmopolitan*. She still wore the shorts and Rolling Stones T-shirt she'd had on the day before, as well as only one sandal. She'd come in after he'd gone to bed, and that was past midnight.

Once dressed, Will went out to start the sprinkler going on the dry grass while he had breakfast. Paige's other sandal lay on the sidewalk. He took it back in the house and threw it into her room before returning to the kitchen to see what, if anything, was in the refrigerator.

No milk. No orange juice. Butter, but no bread. Just because she never ate breakfast. In the freezer was an empty ice tray and a linguini-and-clam-sauce Diet Dinner. Even if he had time, he wouldn't eat that. Not at gunpoint.

It looked like cold pizza for breakfast. Again. One of the side benefits of working for Pizza on Wheels was that he'd never starve. There were always leftover pizzas from people who ordered them and then changed their minds. Or pizzas that were ordered as jokes for delivery to people who didn't want them. He'd never starve, but he might develop pellagra, or scurvy, or some other nutritional deficiency.

He checked the clock. Seven-fifteen. Paige had a class to teach at eight. On his way to his room to gather his books, he stopped in her doorway.

"Paige. It's seven-fifteen."

She didn't move.

"Paige," he said louder.

She lifted her head, groaned, and dropped it into the pillow again.

"You've got a class at eight."

She groaned again. "Forget it."

"Come on, Paige. You'll lose your job." He closed his mouth before he could add, "Again."

"Call Lars," she muttered into the pillow. "Get him to cover for me."

"You know he won't. He's already too busy with the weight room. There's no way he has time to teach an aerobics class." Will was getting the sinking feeling he always got when he knew it would be up to him to bail her out. "What about Lisa? Maybe she'd switch her nine o'clock for your eight."

Paige lifted her hand, circling the index finger and thumb, then let it fall back onto the bed. He couldn't see her face through the spill of her long dark hair, but he'd bet her eyes were closed.

He threw his books on the kitchen table, searched among the numbers written on the wall beside the phone until he found Lisa's and dialed. Of course, he woke her up. She wasn't happy about it, but she agreed to make the switch. Paige wins again, Will thought.

Back in her bedroom, he said to her inert body, "I'm setting the alarm for eight. You better get up. And don't forget to go to the store today. The cupboards are bare. Paige? Are you listening?"

She grunted.

"I'm going to school now. You get up at eight, okay?"

"Okay, okay," she said, coming up on her elbow and glaring at him over her shoulder. "Go to school already and let me get some sleep."

Will loaded his backpack, wheeled his bike through the front door and down the two porch steps, stopping to turn off the sprinkler, and started for school. A Santa Ana wind was blowing from the east. It would be another hot day, and so dry his skin already felt parched. A good beach day, even in mid-October. He always thought school shouldn't start in Imperial Beach until November. Summer hung on for a long time in Southern California.

He knew he'd feel cooked by the time he got to school, and worse when he arrived at Pizza on Wheels this afternoon. At least the delivery van was air-conditioned. Something to look forward to. That, and weekends. He worked from three to eleven, and sometimes later, on weekdays, and that was enough. Weekends were his own.

Tomorrow was Saturday and he was going to spend the whole day at the beach. He loved the beach. He'd grown up almost on the sand. The ramshackle cottage his parents had bought twenty-one years ago, when Paige was on the way, was one of a string of such houses just above the Mexican border, cheap because of the proximity to Tijuana's poverty, periodic sewage overflows, and constant population of illegal aliens trudging up the beach past the Griffins' house.

Now the house belonged to him and Paige alone, the last thing their mother had to leave them when she died of emphysema two years before. Their father hadn't left them anything when he'd taken off for parts unknown just after Will was born. Not even a photograph. Will had no memory of him.

The Santa Ana was still blowing early Saturday morning when Will scrambled over the riprap in front of the house to reach the beach. He could smell the desert on the wind, dry and hot.

He liked to be on the beach with the early people: the dog walkers and surfers, grandmothers with little kids, and shell gatherers—people who didn't want to sleep the morning away. The kids were great to watch. They reminded Will of how he used to be, the way they squatted at the tide line digging with plastic shovels, their feet buried in the sand, watching sand crabs scuttle sideways into the surf.

A black dog came down the beach from the north, prancing and proud, as if he knew he wasn't supposed to be there without a leash and an owner, but didn't care. His pink tongue lolled sideways out of his grinning mouth, and Will grinned back. He knew just how the dog felt.

The dog stopped where two small boys were digging in the sand and watched them. One of the boys patted the dog, who, with placid dignity, stood still for it. Then the dog turned to the ocean as if just noticing it, and his ears lifted.

Will could almost feel the dog's muscles gathering tension, preparing themselves. With a rush, the dog ran to the water's edge and threw himself joyously into the surf. He leapt, sending a spray of silver drops into the air, turned and ran, dripping, back onto the sand, a foaming wave chasing him.

Just as the wave exhausted itself, the dog reversed and pursued it, through sucking sand, to where it folded back into the sea. He plunged after it, swiveled, and repeated the game.

On the dog's third bound into the water, Will joined him, not bothering to even strip off his sleeveless sweatshirt. The dog turned his grinning face to Will and kept going, swimming out a few feet, then waiting for Will to catch up. Hot white sunlight splintered in the water around them and glittered on the dog's wet head. Will laughed out loud, and the two of them swam back to the beach, pushed by an incoming wave.

The sun was higher in the sky by several degrees before they were tired enough to quit. Will threw his sopping sweatshirt onto the sand and dropped, stomach-down, onto it as the dog shook himself again and again. Then, stopping long enough to lick Will's ear, he trotted away in the direction he had come. Will waved goodbye. "See you tomorrow?" he called.

The beach was empty; the early occupants had gone in for breakfast, the serious sun-seekers had not yet arrived. Will dozed on the hot sand, the sting of salt and sun an agreeable sensation on his shoulders, until he was too hungry to wait any longer to eat. When he came back later, the beach would be different, no longer his own as it was in the early morning.

He left his sweatshirt on the back-porch railing and wiped his sandy feet in the patchy grass. Paige was at the kitchen table, her cheek propped on her palm, staring glassily into a cup of coffee, when he came through the back door. Without raising her head, she said, "You smell like seaweed."

"I like it," Will said, putting bread into the toaster. Bread meant orange juice and, he hoped, soap, too. "You should try it."

"Salt water makes my hair sticky."

"It's good for your complexion. I haven't had a zit in months." He poured a tall glass of orange juice, drank it, and poured another.

"That must be why you have such an active social life."

She lit a cigarette and dropped the match into her coffee cup, where it sizzled out.

"If yours is the standard, I'll never be able to match it." He removed his toast from the toaster and buttered it. "I wish you'd stop smoking. At least in the house."

"My habits are none of your business. Neither's my social life." She raised her head and blew smoke at him.

"Yeah?" he asked, sliding his plate onto the table and sitting opposite her. "Who else is going to look out for you? Not any of those flaky friends of yours."

She just looked at him, her head tipped to the side. He liked it better when she argued. When she was quiet, and had that confused expression, he worried. It meant she was thinking and that was always dangerous.

She exhaled a long stream of smoke and dropped her cigarette into the coffee. "You could be right, little brother. You're dependable, if nothing else."

"I'm plenty else." His toast was gone and he got up to make more. While he waited for it, he poured a soup bowl full of Froot Loops, drowned them in milk, and stood at the counter eating.

Her chair screeched as she pushed it back, rose, and wandered toward the hall.

"What are you doing today?" he called after her.

"I'm going to the desert. Lars has a new thing, a dune buggy or something, he wants to play with."

"The desert? You've got to be kidding. It'll be blowing like crazy there, and hotter than it is here."

"So? It's something to do." Her voice faded as she continued down the hall. "I'm thinking of quitting my job."

When she said that, it usually meant she'd already been

fired. He tried to make his voice neutral, though loud enough to be heard, when he said, "How come?"

The bathroom door slammed.

There was a certain place on the beach where the kids from Will's class congregated, and he spent the afternoon there with them. Things weren't quite the same with Jay, his best friend, since he'd started going steady with a girl who, in Will's opinion, was so manipulative she ought to be running a South American country, but he still liked Jay better than anybody else at school. The girl was just a sophomore and she detracted from Will's pleasure in sharing his senioritis with Jay. But the sun was hot, the water cold, there was a portable stereo and a cooler of soft drinks, so the afternoon was all right.

People started leaving about four, but Will stayed. He pulled on a T-shirt and sat in the sand, watching the light change on the water. Next to early morning on the beach, he liked the coming of night best. He hoped the black dog would come back, but he didn't.

Saturday Night Live was almost over when Paige came home. Will was slumped on the couch, his bare feet on the coffee table, a can of Classic Coke balanced on his chest, when he heard her key in the lock.

She threw her purse on top of the television and came to sit next to him. Her face was sunburned and her hair tangled.

"Have fun?" he asked.

"Yeah. The desert has its own austere beauty."

He sat up straighter, grabbing the Coke can to keep it from spilling. "Huh?"

"There's a quality of light there you don't see anywhere else."

"Who have you been talking to? That doesn't sound like Lars." He tried to get a sniff of her breath. She had both shoes on.

"The people who live in the desert are different," she said abstractedly. "More inner-directed. More self-sufficient."

He shrugged. "Could be."

She looked at him from the corners of her eyes. "I wouldn't mind living there myself."

"You? There's no shopping malls, no places to go dancing. No beach."

"Plenty of sand, though. And clean air, and time to discover yourself."

"You sure you want to get into that?" He knew all the signs. She was at it again, searching and restless, looking for the place, the man, the job that would make life perfect.

"I'm sure. I took a job in Agua Seca. Waitressing at the Snakebite Café. I start Monday."

"I don't think that's a very good idea," he said, easing into what he was sure would turn out to be a major argument.

"Oh, you're such a wet blanket. Why isn't it a good idea?"

He forgot about easing. He was furious. "You know I can't keep this place going by myself and go to school, too. We barely scrape by with both our incomes. Anyway, you'd go nuts from boredom in a month out there."

"The job only lasts until June 1. The Snakebite closes in the summer because it's too hot. I can do anything that long. Besides," she said, smiling placidly, "they need a cook, and since I'm your legal guardian and you have to go with me, I told them you'd take the job."

2

Paige left Sunday afternoon, her car loaded with plastic bags and grocery sacks full of her belongings, a pile of fashion magazines on the floor of the front seat, along with the old fast-food wrappers that were always there. She would move into the trailer behind the Snakebite Café, the trailer which would be their new home, and return for Will once he had rented the beach house.

He stood, watching her car make the last turn out of sight, and didn't lift his hand in farewell. He was exhausted from lack of sleep and from hot, frustrated rage. He didn't even want to go back into the house. It seemed to still vibrate with the argument that had gone on until almost dawn, until both of them were too drained to do more than glare at each other.

After too few hours of sleep, he'd gone to stand by Paige's bed, where she lay, still dressed, her face in the pillow, and had woken her by saying, "You've wised up now, right?"

She'd lifted her head and said, "Give it a rest. I'm going. You can do what you want."

She knew he had no choice. He didn't want to drop out of school, be declared an emancipated minor by the court and go to work full-time. He was determined to finish high school. Not just because he'd promised his mother he would; he wanted to. He even had a dream of getting to college someday.

"Paige, this is crazy. You'll hate the desert. There's nothing there."

She sat cross-legged on the bed and pushed her hair out of her eyes. "How do you know what I want?"

"Do *you* know?"

"I know I don't want what's here anymore. I'm sick of two-bit jobs and guys who are all hands and no brains, and living in a house where everything's always damp. I haven't had a crisp cracker in years."

Will surprised himself by laughing. "You're dragging us off to live nowhere so you can have crisp crackers?"

"I need a change."

"You change all the time. Jobs, men, the color of your hair. I want to stay here and finish school."

"There's a high school there. Somewhere."

He rolled his eyes and went on, marshaling the same arguments he'd used the night before, as if daylight gave them a force they hadn't had before. Paige was unmoved. He followed her, reasoning, pleading, yelling, while she wandered through the house, tossing her things into bags, a succession of cigarettes stuck in the corner of her mouth. She didn't bother to respond to him anymore, and he was slow to realize it was because she had stopped listening.

Now he went back into the house and stood in the doorway of her bedroom, looking at the tangle of hangers on the closet floor, the rumpled bed, the dust bunnies in the corners. More like dust elephants, he thought sourly. I wonder how she'll like having sand dunes in the house.

He smacked his fist against the doorframe and went into the living room, where he snapped on the TV and dropped onto the couch.

A football game played before his eyes, but the space behind them was busy with other concerns: locating a renter for the house, finding out about the new high school, quitting his job at Pizza on Wheels. How did Paige always manage to slip through the complications of real life, leaving the mess for him?

He looked at his watch. Four o'clock on Sunday afternoon. A whole day, when he could have been at the beach, wasted on Paige. He stood, shucked his shorts and T-shirt on the living-room floor, grabbed his bathing suit from the shower rod in the bathroom, and pulled it on as he made his way through the kitchen to the back door. He snagged a towel from the clothesline, negotiated the riprap, and jogged down the beach to the gathering place.

When he got there, almost everybody had already gone or was in the process of packing up to leave. Only Jay still lay, dozing on his stomach, his sophomore girlfriend's head resting in the small of his back.

"Hi," Will said.

Jay opened one eye. "Where you been, buddy?"

"Duking it out with Paige." Will threw his towel in the sand, scattering some onto the perfectly tan legs of Jay's girl, and sat. The girl, whose name Will refused to remember, frowned at him, brushed off her legs, and closed her eyes again.

"Don't you ever learn?" Jay asked. "She's got your number."

"You should talk."

The girl opened her eyes briefly, and so did Jay. "Careful, buddy. Don't take your problems with Paige out on me. What's she doing now?"

"It's too bizarre. Come over and I'll tell you all about it."

The girl sat up and began gathering her beach equipment—sunscreen, towels, visor, trashy paperback—into her bag. "Jay and I are having dinner together," she said to Will.

"How long does that take?" he asked.

"As long as I want it to." She stood, slung her bag over her shoulder, and began walking up the beach.

"Hey, Tammy, wait!" Jay called after her, scrambling to find his flip-flops, shirt, and watch. "What's with the two of you?" he said to Will.

"And you think Paige jerks *me* around."

"Tammy!" Jay called again, starting after her. "I'll call you later, or something," he said over his shoulder to Will.

"Or something," Will muttered. "Great. My life's falling apart and my best friend has to go sniffing after some . . ." He raised his head in time to see the black dog racing toward him from up the beach. He got to his feet. "Hey!" he shouted to the dog.

The dog ran past him straight into the surf, and Will followed. Together, they plunged into the cold water, both hurling themselves against the waves. They swam out past the breakers, the dog barking once, sharply, in pure joy.

After their swim, Will and the dog went back to where Will had left his towel. He dried himself and then the dog, who stood patiently, tolerating the attention. Will sat in the sand and the dog lowered himself onto the wet towel.

"Santa Ana's broken," Will said. "Wind's from the west now. Cooler and damper. Did you notice?" He looked at the dog, who grinned back at him. "You're new around here, aren't you? But you love it the same way I do, I can tell." He reached for the dog's tags to read his name, but the dog, as if guarding his anonymity, got to his feet and pranced a few steps away. Then he came closer, licked Will's hand with an apologetic air, and trotted off. He stopped once, looked back, and kept going.

Will felt cold for the first time in days. Time to go in. As he climbed the riprap, he wondered how many more times he'd do that before he left.

3

Will never expected things would move so fast. On Monday he mentioned to Chuck, the assistant manager at Pizza on Wheels, that he was trying to rent his house, and Chuck, newly married and living with his in-laws, was interested. Chuck came home with him after work to have a look and on Tuesday told him he'd take it. Would it be okay if they moved in on the weekend? Will even agreed to leave his bike for Chuck to ride to work.

Wednesday, Will's guidance counselor told him Anza Valley High School, population about three hundred, was nearly thirty miles from Agua Seca, but there was nothing any closer. That's all she knew about it.

Thursday was his last day of work at Pizza on Wheels, and he came home at midnight exhausted, his head feeling as heavy as a bowling ball. Paige was coming for him the next night and he had to get packed and clean up the house.

After fantasizing for so long about what it would be like to live without Paige, he was surprised at how empty the house had seemed with her and her things gone. He was used to her clutter, the music from her radio, the smell of her perfume. Those things had always been there, even when she wasn't, and now the air in the house seemed lifeless without her. She had an aura of something about to happen, and she wasn't afraid of anything, even when she should have been. At her best, she was funny and appealing, and he missed her. He wanted to kick himself.

Will took a Coke from the refrigerator and, carrying it and a large plastic trash bag, shuffled to his bedroom. He took his clothes from the closet, hangers and all, and deposited them in the trash bag. Then he emptied his drawers into it, too. He put his books and shoes into a cardboard box, undressed, and went to bed. Because the trailer in Agua Seca was fully furnished, dishes and linens included, everything else in the house was to be left for Chuck and his bride. Tomorrow after school he'd dust and vacuum, and that would be it. The house he'd always lived in would be somebody else's.

Jay rode home with him after school, pedaling slowly along, single file. They left their bikes in the front yard, and Jay ran the vacuum cleaner while Will dusted. Then, barefoot, they walked on the beach.

"Man, it's not the moon," Jay told him. "It's only about two hours away."

"Yeah. I know. It just seems like the moon. Probably looks like it, too."

"You've never been there?"

"Nope. Have you?"

"Couple of times. It's . . . big."

"That's like motels that advertise they're clean. It's what you say when there's nothing better you can think of. Motels are supposed to be clean. Deserts are supposed to be big."

Jay grinned. "I guess you're right. It'll be different, anyway."

"God, I'm going to miss the water. First thing I do every morning is look out at it. It's never the same. I think about all that life going on underneath it, things I'll never know about. I think about how far it stretches and how somebody on some other continent is probably watching it just like I am at that very same moment. It gives me a weird feeling, like I'm connected to other people, just by water."

"Well, you know what I think about it," Jay said.

"What?"

"It's big."

Will laughed and dug his hands deeper into the pockets of his shorts. "I'll miss y— this." As long as he and Jay had known each other, they had only talked seriously about small things: beer, baseball, cars. The really serious things, they'd shied away from, each hoping the other would understand without words.

"You'll be back. Not even ole Paige can keep you away from the ocean forever."

"We've got to stick together. We haven't got anybody else. Anyway, she's my guardian until I'm eighteen. It's stay with her or go to a foster home."

"Paige as anybody's guardian is a laugh."

Will never understood why he felt defensive, even at the truth about Paige. "She does what she can."

Jay sighed. "Yeah. Well, none of my business, anyway."

They stood at the water's edge and let the dying waves curl about their feet, excavating moats around them in the sand. "Can I buy you a pizza?" Jay asked.

"How about enchiladas? Pizza is one thing I won't mind leaving behind."

"Okay, enchiladas. We can bring them back here and watch the sunset."

"That'd be good."

Paige arrived at seven-thirty, impatient and annoyed. The air-conditioning in the car was broken and the radiator had boiled over on the grade up out of Agua Seca. She hadn't had dinner and there wasn't anything in the house except Froot Loops and mustard.

"Get your stuff in the car. I want to go."

"Cool it, Paige. Go out for a hamburger while I do the last clean-up around here."

"I don't see why you aren't ready. You knew when I was coming."

"Go get some dinner, Paige. I'm not up for this."

The screen door slammed behind her as she whirled off to her car. Will shook his head at the sound of screeching tires. Living with her had been bumpy enough with their separate activities and interests, which kept them apart most of the time. What would it be like when they had to live and work together in a place where they knew only each other?

It was funny, Will thought, as he put what was left in the medicine chest into a small plastic bag. As long as their mother had been alive, he'd hardly thought about the way Paige lived. That was just Paige and how she did it. There was an adult between him and her to worry and take charge. But after their mother died he realized nobody was in charge, and Paige had never shown any signs of wanting the job, even though she was now twenty and a high-school graduate. She let her laundry pile up for weeks, and while she'd done that and he'd paid no attention when their mother was alive, now it drove him crazy and frightened him. Didn't she have a tight grip on anything? She never paid a bill until two or three late notices had arrived, so Will took over handling their money. If things broke around the house, she ignored them, so Will was the one to fix them, or call someone else to do it. He even did the cooking. She left her dirty dishes all over the place—in the bathroom, next to the telephone—and Will retrieved and washed them before the roaches could find them. Paige never seemed to notice.

She redeemed herself by making him laugh with her imitations of the ladies in her aerobics classes, by leaving notes on his pillow that he found when he came in from Pizza on Wheels (LOOK IN THE FREEZER, and he would find Cookies 'n' Cream, his favorite ice cream, waiting for him), by painting a seascape mural on his bedroom wall one day when he was at school and she was out of work.

Who could tell? Maybe living in the desert was just what she needed to grow up.

Right.

He'd thought that when she started selling lingerie at home parties, and then when she wanted to manufacture jewelry from feathers and pop tops and other beach debris. Why couldn't she get interested in something like teaching underprivileged children, or high finance, or great literature? Why did it always have to be spirit channeling, leotard designing, Tantric massage?

Will knotted the plastic bag and dropped it onto his clothes in the trash bag.

The trash bag and cardboard box waited by the front door while he gave a final swipe of the mop to the kitchen and bathroom floors and locked the back door. He stood in the doorway of his emptied room, remembering, when he heard the screen door bang, and Paige's footsteps come down the hall.

She had to reach up to put her hand on the back of his neck. Their mother always said Paige got all the small, delicate, pretty genes and Will got all the big, sturdy, good-looking ones. He knew she was being generous about his looks, though there was no denying he was big.

"Sorry, little brother. I was hot and hungry. You were right. I needed dinner."

He shrugged.

"Can I help you with your stuff?"

"It's all ready. By the door."

"That's all? My junk filled up the whole car." She rubbed his neck. "You've always been better organized than me."

"No joke," he said.

"Okay, okay. Let's not fight. We've got to spend two hours together in a car with no air-conditioning. If we start fighting now, we'll kill each other before we get to the desert."

"Might save us both a lot of trouble."

She took her hand from his neck and sighed. "You might like it, not that you'd ever tell me if you did, I'm sure."

He turned from her and headed for the front door. "Let's get out of here."

Will fell asleep on the freeway and woke up just as Paige started down the grade into the desert valley. He could see scattered lights on the valley floor, tiny lost points engulfed in blackness, and around them, silhouetted against the dark night sky, the humps and peaks of mountains.

"We'll be there in about thirty minutes," Paige said, concentrating on the snaking curves in the steep road. "Look up. Did you ever see so many stars? There's no city lights to wash them out."

Will rested his head on the open window frame and looked. The stars seemed at once close enough to touch and so far away he couldn't even imagine the immense cold darkness between them and him.

He thought he knew about stars. He'd loved sitting on the beach, watching the stars appear, benign and decorative. Could these be the same stars he'd seen from the beach? There were so many more of them, and they looked colder and harder and more primitive than he remembered. He could even see the foggy brilliance of the Milky Way across the sky, something he'd heard about but doubted really existed.

The sprinkled lights from the valley, drawing closer, seemed a weak reflection of the celestial extravaganza overhead. Alien territory, for sure, he thought.

"Well, what do you think, little brother?"

"Wow," he said, in the most bored voice he could produce.

"What does it take to make an impression on you,

anyway?" she asked. "That sky's spectacular. You have to open yourself to the experience, be willing to see with new eyes, embrace novelty."

"Who the hell has been telling you this stuff?"

"You don't think I can come up with it myself? You think I'm like some kind of puppet, saying somebody else's words? I can figure things out all by myself, you know."

"Speaking of embracing a novelty."

"Oh, shut up."

They drove the rest of the way in silence, their windows open to the warm, sagey smell of the desert.

4

When Paige opened the door to the trailer, a gush of glacial air met them.

"Damn," she said. "I forgot to turn the air-conditioning down. Oh, well. We don't pay for it."

Will found the thermostat and adjusted it. Immediately the trailer became silent as the laboring machine shut off.

Paige dropped her purse on the tiny kitchen table. "There's two bedrooms, but the only closet's in mine. Then there's the living room, the kitchen, and the bathroom. Nice and compact."

Will looked around him. He could see both ends of the trailer from where he stood. It looked like an iron lung. "I'd say compact was the exact right word." He went out to the car to get his things. The desert night felt unpleasantly hot after the refrigerated trailer.

"I'm going to bed," Paige called after him. "We have to be at the Snakebite at six. It opens at six-thirty."

"A.m.?"

"Of course a.m. People start early around here, when it's cooler. They hole up in the middle of the day. I'll get you up in time."

He wondered how long it would take before her enthusiasm for early rising wore off and he'd be the one trying to get her out of bed.

Just like her to leave him with the unloading, he thought, hauling in the trash bag. And to be shut up in her room, where the only closet is, so I can't hang anything up. And to expect me to start cooking when I've never even laid eyes on the kitchen I'm supposed to be cooking in. Yes sir, Paige is really ready to change.

A narrow bed and a small bureau took up most of the space in Will's room. When he sat on the end of the bed, he could reach the bureau drawers, which he filled with as much as he could. He hung some things on a hook behind the door, and piled the rest on the brown tweed love seat in the living room. He left his door open when he got into bed. With it shut, there didn't seem to be enough of the icy air in his room to supply more than three or four breaths.

The bed was too short for him and the sheets smelled musty. He felt as if he'd just closed his eyes when Paige was shaking him awake.

"Rise and shine, sleeping beauty. It's quarter to six. We can eat at the Snakebite."

He dressed and followed her across the strip of sandy soil between the trailer and the back door of the café. Around the sides of the Snakebite, all Will could see were a gas station next door and lots of desert. Was this all there was to Agua Seca?

Paige unlocked the door and flipped on the lights, revealing a long, narrow room with a counter running the length of it. Several tables lined the other wall, under big windows shaded by metal awnings. The windows gave a view of the highway. The grill behind the counter was in full view of all the customers.

Paige started two pots of coffee while Will tried to

figure out how to turn the grill on. Once he got it going, he opened the big refrigerator and found it crammed with cartons of juice, milk, pancake batter, packages of hamburger meat, piles of cheese squares separated by leaves of paper, plastic bags full of steaks, slabs of bacon, flats of eggs, sacks of raw french fries, blocks of butter. The crispers held heads of iceberg lettuce and big red tomatoes.

"I think I've got the menu figured out," he said, tying a dish towel around his waist. "Who stocked up?" He doubted it had been Paige.

"The owner. Before he left yesterday," Paige said absently, pouring herself some coffee. "Want some?"

"You know I can't stand coffee." He poured himself a glass of orange juice while he located the toaster and the drawers filled with bread loaves; also the cooler stocked with beer and soft drinks. A wire rack with a Kellogg's logo held single servings of various cereals.

Paige slapped silverware on tables and along the counter, filled cream pitchers from a carton, and turned on the radio to a country-and-Western station. "Make me some toast, would you, little brother? You might as well get in practice."

"You know I can only do this on weekends," Will said, putting two slices of bread into the toaster. "I'll be going to school the rest of the time."

"No problem," Paige said. "Most of the business is on the weekends anyway, when the city folks come to play with their ATVs. We're closed Monday and Tuesday. I can handle what midweek business there is. We close at three then, anyhow."

"What's an ATV?" He buttered her toast, cleaved it in

half with a huge knife, and slid it down the counter to her.

"All-terrain vehicle. You'll see."

At six-thirty Paige unlocked the front door and turned the cardboard sign in it around so the OPEN faced out. A tall man in cowboy boots came in, seated himself at a table by the window, and ordered coffee, eggs, and potatoes. Then he pulled a piece of wood and a short knife from his pocket, spread out a napkin to receive the shavings, and began to whittle.

Carefully, Will cut off a piece of butter and put it on the grill. He broke and scrambled eggs, poured them onto the melted butter, then emptied part of a bag of potatoes into a puddle of oil he'd poured from a plastic pitcher. He stirred the eggs, flipped the potatoes, and stuck toast into the toaster. Everything got done at roughly the same time, and with only a small amount of uncertainty he got the toast, eggs, and potatoes onto a plate and over to Paige to deliver. He felt as if he'd done a day's work. If the café ever filled up, he was a goner. He'd done plenty of cooking since his mother died, but never for a lot of people at once.

A woman in a long, gray skirt, carrying a Bible under her arm, came in and sat at the counter. "Morning, Sam," she said, swiveling her stool so she faced the man by the window.

He nodded to her and kept eating.

She turned back and beamed at Paige. Paige smiled and said, "Hi, Truline. Meet my brother, Will."

"Hallelujah," Truline said. "Flapjacks and sausage, please, dear, and a cup of tea, if you don't mind."

Will rummaged in the refrigerator until he found an

unopened package of sausages. He threw four onto the grill and let them cook for a few minutes before he poured out the pancake batter. He liked the way almost everything was within arm's reach of the cook. Whoever had arranged the kitchen knew what he was doing. He was grateful, too, that the menu had been kept simple.

When Paige delivered Truline's breakfast to her, Truline raised her teacup in Will's direction and said, "Thank you, Willie dear, for my daily flapjacks." She giggled, a young sound from her old face. "I always liked flapjacks better than bread. I don't suppose the Good Lord minds."

Will couldn't help smiling. Was it possible Truline was the one responsible for Paige's sudden need to live in the desert? If so, this might be a real turning point.

"Welcome, ma'm," Will said.

"Paige told me her little brother was coming. Don't think anybody could truthfully call you little, though."

"No, ma'm," Will said, scraping sausage fat off the grill.

"Well, like it says in Matthew, 'He who is greatest among you shall be your servant.' You're surely the largest among us, and you're cooking for us. Everything that has and is and ever will happen is all in the Book."

"Yes, ma'm."

"I swan, these are the best flapjacks I ever tasted. You have to tell me your secret. How did you make these?"

"I just poured them out onto the griddle. Nothing to it."

"Well, they're so light, and just the right color, not too dark and not too pale. You are a fine cook, Paige's little brother."

"Thanks."

The tall man by the window finished his breakfast and

pushed his plate aside so he could take up his whittling again. He glanced at Will and raised an eyebrow. Will thought he saw the ends of a smile beneath the man's thick mustache.

Suddenly, it seemed, the place was full of people. A glance through the window showed Will what must be ATVs, towed behind trucks and four-wheel drives crammed into the parking lot. For the next hour he was too busy throwing things on the grill, trying to keep straight which order the bacon went with and which the sausage, looking for clean utensils and more bread, and failing to make everything on the same order finish cooking at the same time.

The customers didn't mind. They were relaxed and jovial, looking forward to a day in the desert, talking too loud, laughing too much. They hardly noticed when their meals were slow to arrive, with the wrong food on the wrong plates. They all seemed to know each other and they cheerfully switched things around.

Will had to keep mopping his face with his apron to avoid sweating on the food. The air-conditioning in the café seemed completely ineffective behind the counter. Even Paige, who was sweat-free at the end of a ninety-minute aerobics class, had beads on her upper lip and dark rings under her arms.

The ATVers left as suddenly as they'd arrived, leaving generous tips. One young man with a blond ponytail and the face of an archangel leaned over the counter and gave Paige a long kiss on the cheek before he went.

"See you tonight, pretty Paige," he said. "I'll show you blameless, dancing stars."

Will, watching the color rise in Paige's cheeks, revised

his notion that Truline might be the magnet drawing Paige to this place.

Truline, her breakfast long finished, sat drinking endless cups of increasingly weaker tea and watching the crowd, smiling and nodding gently. When the young man kissed Paige, Truline lowered her eyes and murmured, "Oh, that you would kiss me with the kisses of your mouth." Then she giggled.

At nine-thirty, the only people left in the Snakebite besides Will and Paige were Truline and the whittler Truline had called Sam. The kitchen area behind the counter was a shambles of broken eggshells, pancake-batter drips, bacon spatters, and dirty plates. Will's shirt was soaked through and he was ready to head for the trailer and a nap. How was he ever going to work until eight o'clock, the Friday and Saturday closing hour?

Truline picked up her Bible and wiggled her fingers to Paige and Will in farewell. "Why don't you and Timothy come to the prayer meeting tonight, Paige?" she asked, sliding off her stool. "Bring Willie, too."

"We'll see," Paige told her.

When Truline left, Will turned to Paige. "Blameless, dancing stars? Give me a break."

Paige busily wiped the counter, depositing dirty dishes into the plastic tub under the sink, and said nothing.

"Timothy wouldn't, by any chance, be one of those self-sufficient, inner-directed types who appreciates the desert's austere beauty, would he?"

"What if he is? What's wrong with that?"

"I bet there's nothing austere about the way you appreciate him. I can't believe you dragged me out here for one of your passing infatuations."

"You don't know anything about anything. I can get a new start here." She seemed close to tears.

"This isn't how you do that." He lowered his voice. "It doesn't depend on somebody else."

"Let me live my own way! You're supposed to be my friend."

He turned his hands out helplessly. "I am your friend. You know I—"

She spun away from him and ran out the back door.

He turned to the grill, his shoulders slumped, and began scraping crusts of burned stuff off with his spatula. The silence in the room was broken only by the soft sound of the whittler's knife against wood. Will was embarrassed when he realized the man had heard everything he and Paige had said to each other. He sneaked a glance at the man and caught his eye for an instant before they both looked away. Once again, he thought he saw the suggestion of a smile beneath the mustache.

The man laid his knife and his piece of wood on the table and ambled over to the counter.

"Can I help you?" Will asked.

"Thought maybe I could help you," he said.

"How do you mean?"

"Thought maybe I could offer you something else to do tonight besides going to Truline's prayer meeting."

Will looked down at the dirty spatula in his hand. "What did you have in mind?"

"How'd you like to come by my place for a beer and some talk? It ain't much for a Saturday night, but then, there ain't much around here to offer. Too, I reckon drinking a beer with a geezer like me's a sight better than thumping Bibles for an hour."

Will looked up. "I'm not interested in thumping Bibles, whatever that means, even for a minute."

"Guess you're not much for taking in those blameless, dancing stars, either."

Will grinned. "You know that guy?"

"I know everybody around here."

"Yeah, okay. A beer sounds good. You don't happen to have one on you right now, do you?"

"You'll need one worse by tonight, boy. Come on over after closing, then. I'm down the road east about a mile and a half. Double trailer under a tamarisk tree. Says Sam Webb over the door. That's my name."

"Nice coincidence," Will said.

Sam Webb was laughing, walking back to his table, when Paige returned.

She didn't look at Sam or Will, just collected more dirty dishes and stacked them haphazardly in the giant dishwasher.

Sam dropped some coins on his table, picked up his wood and knife, and went out the door, holding it open for a girl in baggy khaki shorts and a black T-shirt who was coming in. "Morning, honey," he said.

"Hi, Sam."

She took a seat at the counter and said to Will, "I'll have a Belgian waffle and some fresh strawberries. Cup of *café au lait* and a glass of Perrier."

"I think you've got this place confused with somewhere real," he said. "We've got hotcakes, orange juice, Maxwell House, and tap water."

"Yeah, I know," she said. "I was just testing the new cook. Well, I guess the excitement's over for today. I'll settle for Rice Krispies and scrambled eggs. Don't tell me they're unborn chickens. And I'll have some orange juice."

"Unborn chickens?"

"That's what my mother always says. She's big on not eating dead things."

"I guess I won't be seeing her in here, then," Will said, breaking eggs into a bowl. "That refrigerator's full of dead things."

Paige slouched at the end of the counter, staring into a coffee cup.

Will dropped a box of Rice Krispies into a bowl and put it in front of the girl. She lifted her long, brown hair off her neck in a cooling gesture, and Will saw that she was wearing big rhinestone earrings.

He watched her open the cereal box with clean, precise movements. Her fingers were long and slender and her wrists were tiny. All of her was small, too small for the loose clothing she was wearing. She looked like a child in her mother's clothes and jewelry.

"You're looking at my earrings, aren't you?" she asked, when he brought her eggs.

"What makes you think so?"

"I can tell. Every time I wear these, somebody makes a smart remark about them."

"How come you keep wearing them if they cause you so much trouble?"

"I'll wear whatever I damn well please."

Will blinked, surprised by her sudden combativeness. "Then you better quit worrying about what other people think. Unless you're using those earrings as an excuse for a fight." He was in no mood to be hassled by her.

"I guess you're not expecting a big tip," the girl said, shoveling unborn chickens into her mouth.

"I don't want any tip if it means you're paying me to shut up."

"I probably don't have enough money to do that."

"You probably don't." He turned his back to her and rearranged the dishes Paige had dumped in the dishwasher. He was conscious of the sweat stains on his shirt.

Against the background of country-and-Western music, he could hear the clink of her spoon against her bowl. It was a fast, hard clink, and listening to it, he didn't have any trouble interpreting her state of mind.

He heard the creak of her stool as she stood up, her quick footsteps and the slam of the front door, its bell jangling. He turned to find she had left the exact amount of the check, in piles of nickels, dimes, and pennies, next to her plate. No tip. It was as if she'd broken open a piggy bank to pay for her breakfast. She looked like a child and she paid like one. She acted like one, too. He scooped up the coins and took them to the cash register.

"Nice going," Paige said, looking up from her coffee cup. "Drive away the customers and we'll be out of jobs."

"Fine with me." He loaded the girl's dishes into the dishwasher and turned it on.

"Don't start," Paige warned him. "I don't want to hear about it."

Perversely, he kept going. "You know I only came with you because I had a legal and moral obligation to."

"What do you mean, a moral obligation? What am I, some charity you've adopted? You're the one who needs a guardian."

"Not nearly as much as you do."

"Is this the person who's always talking about how we have to stick together, how we have to look out for each other, how we're each other's only family now? I didn't know that meant I was some kind of affliction you had to bear."

"That's not what I mean," he said, aware they were having another pointless argument and looking for a way out of it. "Come on, Paige. Haven't you had enough of this wrangling? We're here, we're here together, let's make the best of it. It's too late to do anything else, anyway. Somebody else is living in our house at the beach, we've burned our bridges. Let's try what you say: open ourselves to a new experience." He never thought he'd be saying stuff like this to Paige. He'd vowed he was going to act offended and wounded until the day they left Agua Seca, never letting her forget that she was the cause of his having to leave a place he loved. Now here he was, suggesting they open themselves up to a new experience. Didn't he have any principles? How could Paige always manage to get him where she wanted him before he even knew what had happened?

She came and put her arms around his waist, resting her head against his chest. "Thank you, Will. I know this move is hard on you, and that you only did it for me. I want you to know how much that means to me. You really are my best friend, even when we're fighting."

His arms hung at his sides, a fork in one hand, a dish towel in the other. "Okay, okay. Let go. I'm too sweaty to hug. Anyway, I've got to clean the grill before the grease burns on it."

5

The ATVers returned at noon for lunch and a rest out of the sun. They ate and drank without stopping, regaling each other with the thrills and spills of the morning. One hamburger called for another. More fries when the first two batches were gone. Lots of beer to wash the sand out of their throats. The heat from the grill assaulted Will, and his sweat dropped and sizzled next to the burgers. He burned batches of fries, forgetting them as he flipped hamburgers; he cut himself slicing tomatoes, and then had trouble cooking with Band-Aids on his fingers.

About three, the crowd left for one last round of whatever they did out there. And then they came back for dinner.

Will was staggering with fatigue at four, and was a zombie by eight, when they closed. He and Paige, moving slowly, cleaned up, washed dishes, and laid out new place settings.

"Did you know it got this busy on the weekends?" Will asked.

"How could I know that? The owner said it was busy, but he didn't say it was wild." Already she sounded sick of the place.

"When does more food get delivered? Those vultures put a big dent in what was in the refrigerator."

"Monday, and again on Friday. You have to make the orders, so you have to keep track of what we run out of."

"Great. I don't even know what we're supposed to have. How do I know when we run out of it?"

"That's your problem. The owner's gone off to the Caribbean for three weeks. He could hardly wait to get out of here."

"He's gone? We're supposed to run everything for three weeks? We don't know what we're doing."

"He said he trusted me. And he said he hadn't been out of the desert in two years. Wouldn't you want to get away, too?"

"I already do." The owner trusted Paige? Who in the world must have been working here before? He later found out: drifters and drunks who never stayed long. Paige must have looked like the answer to a prayer.

When they finished, Will untied his apron and said, "I hope I can stay awake this evening."

"Why do you have to? Just go to bed."

"I'm going to have a beer at Sam Webb's."

"Well, that's nice," she said, brightening. "See? You have a friend already."

"I'm going to get in the shower. Maybe that'll revive me."

"I'll lock up and be right there."

Will crossed from the back door of the Snakebite to the trailer. Once he got inside, he felt as if he'd been sandbagged: he couldn't take another step. He dropped onto the couch, leaned his head back, and was asleep in a second.

When he woke, disoriented, the first sound he heard was the shower.

Paige. She hadn't waked him, even knowing he wanted to shower before she did.

He got up, his head heavy and muddled, and went to hammer on the bathroom door. "Get out of there, Paige."

"What?" she called. "I'll be done in a minute. You looked so sweet and exhausted I didn't have the heart to wake you."

He restrained himself from kicking the door and went to his cubicle of a room, where he pulled off his dirty T-shirt and dropped it on the floor. The shower stopped, and a minute later he heard the door open.

"It's all yours."

As he stepped out of the shower ten minutes later, he heard the crunch of tires on sand and the familiar screech of the fan belt slipping on Paige's car. Damn! He'd figured Timothy would come for her and he could take the car to Sam's. Now he'd have to go on foot in the dark. He'd need another shower by the time he got there if he didn't get eaten by some desert animal, or get lost in the trackless wastes and wander for days without water. He threw his towel on the floor and this time allowed himself to kick the bathroom door.

Just before he left the trailer, he stopped in the bathroom and hung up his towel. And Paige's.

Fortunately, Sam's place wasn't hard to find; there was hardly anything between the Snakebite and it. And Will presumed that his moderate-paced jog had scared off any man-eating animals, but his clean shirt was damp and his shower a waste of time.

The lights from the trailer windows spread lemony squares on the sand. He walked through them as he mounted a curved set of steps to the front door. The noise from the air-conditioner was so loud he wasn't sure his knock would be heard. If he could find any place to put it.

Every inch of the door was carved with scenes of the desert: coyotes chasing roadrunners and vice versa, ocotillo in bloom, kangaroo rats in a conga line, two snakes forming a heart shape—each picture real and funny and original.

While Will was still contemplating where to lay his knuckles, the door opened.

"Thought you might have changed your mind about the prayer meeting," Sam told him.

"No way. I crashed after work and Paige took the car. Sorry if I'm late." He came into the living room.

"Hardly any such thing as late around here," Sam said. "We kind of make our own time. Could you use a beer?"

"Have you got a Coke?"

"Sure."

While Sam went to the kitchen, Will looked around the big square room. It was divided by a floor-to-ceiling row of carved spindles separating a workshop at the end of the trailer from the living area. The floor in the workshop was tile and littered with shavings. A long workbench stretched the width of the room under the windows, bare except for finished and in-progress carvings. Tools hung neatly on the wall.

The living room was unexpectedly pretty, with pale

wall-to-wall carpet, comfortable-looking chairs, and a sofa upholstered in soft desert shades. A cactus garden in baskets filled one corner.

Sam came from the kitchen with a Coke, a beer, and a plate of cheese, fruit, and crackers, as Will lowered himself into a chair. He jumped up again to take the Coke.

Sam pushed the plate toward him. "Sit down. I figured you might not have gotten around to eating today."

As soon as Sam said that, Will realized he was famished. "I guess I didn't," he said, snapping a cracker in two before eating it. "Paige was right about the crackers, anyway."

"How's that?"

"She said she wanted to get away from the ocean and live here so she could have crisp crackers for a change."

Sam laughed. "That's as good a reason as any when a body's restless to move on."

"I guess." Will ate while Sam sat quietly sipping his beer and wiping the foam from his mustache. "What were you carving this morning in the Snakebite?"

Sam went into the workshop and came back with an unfinished figure of an Indian woman weaving a basket. He handed it to Will, who turned it around in his fingers. "It's great. How hard is this to do? It looks complicated."

"Yeah," Sam said. "More interesting that way."

"Because it takes longer?" He handed the figure back to Sam.

"Because it's more interesting. You worried about filling up time around here?" Before Will could think of an answer, Sam asked, "Or are you worrying about something else?"

Will looked up, his mouth full, surprise stamped on his face.

"Well, boy, you look like a worrier to me."

Will swallowed. "It's a dirty job, but somebody's got to do it."

"Unlike whittling, worrying's something that doesn't get easier with practice. You interested in learning to carve? It's better for you."

"Me? I don't think I can."

"Ever try?"

Will shook his head.

"You've got the hands for it. Big and careful. I watched you cook."

Will looked at Sam's hands, turning the Indian figure around and around. They were broad and brown and could have been made from the same wood as the figure. "Could you teach me?"

"I'm willing if you are."

Will shrugged. "Why not?" He was studying his own hands, wondering what made them look careful in spite of the Band-Aids, when the front door opened and a voice called, "Sam?"

"Come on in, Mike," Sam said, setting the Indian figure on the table beside his chair.

Will looked up into the face of the girl from the Snakebite. She still wore the baggy khaki shorts and black T-shirt.

"Oh," she said. "I didn't know you had company."

"Mike, this is Will Griffin. Will, Mike Macey."

Will opened his mouth to say something. He wasn't sure what it was going to be, and he never got a chance to find out.

"Yes, it's Mike," she said. "It's not short for Michelle or Michaela or anything like that. It says Mikel on my birth certificate. My mother was so sure I'd be a boy she already had things monogrammed Mike, and my mother never changes her mind. Satisfied?"

Will closed his mouth. No point in trying to make conversation with this person. What she wanted was a fight, and he was too tired. He held his hand up in front of him. "Sorry I asked," he said.

"You were going to. Everybody does. I should wear a sign."

"The sign you should wear," Will said, "is 'Stop in for an Argument.' "

"Hey, you two," Sam interjected. "Take it easy. I didn't know you were coming by tonight, Mike. I thought you got enough footage last week." Only then did Will notice Mike was carrying a video camera that seemed half her size. He was damned if he'd ask her what it was for.

"After I edited what I had, I decided I wanted more of your sketches and blueprints. I'll call you about it tomorrow." She turned on the heel of her dirty white tennis shoe and left, closing the door firmly, just this side of a slam.

"What's *her* problem?" Will asked when she was gone. "She was in the Snakebite this morning acting the same way, like she's mad at the world."

"I guess that's her problem," Sam said. "Her mom's an anthropologist, been here about a year working on a dig up some canyon or other. Mike wants to be a documentary filmmaker, but one documentary she doesn't want to make is her mother digging up Indian bones and pottery. And that's what Marcella Macey bought her the video camera for. So Mike's mad at Marcella for dragging her to Sand Land, as she calls it; Marcella's mad at Mike because she won't do as she's told; and just generally nothing they can do pleases the other one."

"Mike wants to make movies? How old is she, twelve?"

"Just turned seventeen. About the same as twelve some days, though. She'll be out of here next fall to go to college no matter what Marcella's doing, but Mike doesn't think she'll last till next fall."

"I know the feeling," Will said.

"How come you're all in such a hurry to get out there and let the world knock you around?"

"You don't have to be out there, wherever that is," Will said, "to get knocked around. Sometimes it begins at home. Like charity."

Sam gave Will a steady look and let out a long breath. "Well, I know that. I just keep forgetting, since I didn't get knocked around at all until I was well grown. I loved being a kid, knowing somebody else was in charge, looking out for things, and all I had to do was go to school and have a good time and postpone being a grownup as long as I could. Just when I thought I might get away with it forever, life kicked me in the teeth."

Will wanted to ask what had happened, but didn't know how.

Before he could frame a response, Sam went on. "Well, it wasn't any worse than what happens to a lot of people and not near as bad as what happens to some. But I thought I was immune, so the shock was worse." He put his beer down. "Why don't we start those carving lessons right now?" He got up and headed toward the workshop. Will jumped to his feet and followed.

"Anything special you'd like to start with?" Sam asked.

"Gee, I don't know. I never thought about it. What did you start with?"

"First thing I ever carved," Sam said, rummaging in a drawer, "was an eagle on a tree limb. I'm the only one who knew what it was. Nobody else could tell if it was a molehill or a vase of flowers or a spavined horse."

"Yeah? How did you get so good?"

"Like I told you. Practice. And I liked doing it, even though I was so bad. Here." He handed Will a lump of something and a knife with a short, curved blade.

"What's this?"

"Beeswax. That's what you begin with. When you've hacked it up too bad to go on, you can melt it down and start all over. It's easier to work on than wood, too. Gives your hands a chance to toughen up. Whittling'll wear you out at first, until your hands get strong."

Will held the lump of beeswax, cool and slightly greasy, in his palm. He liked the heft of it and he liked the feel of the slender knife handle in his other hand. It seemed to fit his fingers exactly.

"What's the difference between whittling and carving?" Will asked.

"Mostly how important it sounds. Like the difference between lawyer and attorney, or teacher and professor. Whittling's what I do. Figures, some funny things, like my front door. Nothing I don't want to do. Carving's furniture and staircases and choir lofts in cathedrals. Stuff you get commissioned to do. I like being the only one who tells me what to do."

"Oh. What do I do with this now?" He held out the lump of beeswax.

"You decide what you want to make. Then you draw a pattern that you can either transfer onto your block of wood—or beeswax, in this case—or just refer to as you go along, and then you start in. That's it. And every cut you do makes you better than you were before."

"Okay. I'll try a dog sitting on his haunches." Will put the beeswax and knife down on the worktable, accepted a pencil and paper from Sam, and sat down to draw a dog.

"Hey!" Will said, surprised. "It looks like a dog sitting on his haunches."

"You're a natural," Sam said. "You've got to see it in your mind before you can get it to come out your fingers. You've got a good visual mind. Look how you got one ear cocked up. Only somebody who's looked at a dog and really seen him can get in a detail like that. See what you can do in the wax. Get comfortable."

Will wasn't sure if that cocked ear was on purpose or an accident, but he liked Sam's thinking he had a good visual mind. He arranged himself in a chair and began gingerly shaving off slivers of wax, referring now and then to his drawing. Sam settled down, too, with his Indian figure, and they worked together, only the sounds of wood and wax falling in curls to the floor in counterpoint to the hum of the air conditioner.

After thirty minutes, Will's hands were cramping and his lump of beeswax looked as if it had tangled with a food processor.

"Ready to quit?" Sam asked.

"I'd better, if I'm going to be able to flip burgers tomorrow. I already feel like the Claw."

"Soak your hands in hot water when you get home.

That'll help. Poking them in and out of the sand helps, too. The abrasiveness toughens them and the heat soothes them. Old desert-rat trick."

"I'll try it." Will put the wax and the knife down on the worktable. "I don't think I have much talent for this."

"Too soon to tell. You're just figuring out how it feels. Did you like it at all?"

"Yeah, I did. I liked the sound of the knife on the wax and the smell of wood around me. Maybe I should learn to make toothpicks out of telephone poles."

Sam laughed. "It doesn't sound odd to me. Those are some of the things I like about it, too. And that's what keeps you doing it. You can have the wax and the knife to take home, if you like."

Will hesitated. "No. I think I'll leave them here. If you don't mind me coming back."

"Suits me. One thing I came to the desert for was solitude, but you can OD on anything, even good stuff."

"Okay." Will rubbed his palms down the sides of his jeans. "Thanks. I guess I'd better get home. The Snakebite opens early. But you know that."

"Take it easy on the way home," Sam said, walking him to the door. "Don't run into any coyotes."

"Might I?" Will turned, hoping he didn't sound as cowardly as he felt.

"They're out there, but they're not interested in you. They got chasing rabbits and howling at the moon on their minds."

"Well, okay. See you." When the door closed behind him, Will had to fight an urge to pound on it and beg to be let back in. The big night outside Sam's trailer seemed dark and dangerous.

The light of the half-moon washed the landscape in silver, interrupted by long black shadows cast from every hump in the terrain. Will's footsteps on the sand seemed unnaturally loud once he was out of earshot of Sam's air conditioner, and he was sure that every inhabitant of the desert, each of them no doubt poisonous and short-tempered, would know exactly where he was.

He stopped walking and just listened. The silence was so intense he thought he could hear the blood flowing through his head. He'd never heard such silence; the absence of sound seemed almost a vast, sucking roar.

Always before, he'd had the rhythm and rush of the sea in his ears—if not loud enough to actually hear, at least close enough to feel its pull. Now it was barely possible for him to believe there was such a thing as an ocean. He stood in a sea of sand, a foreign, inhospitable place, where water of any sort was a secret, where silence seemed to grow in time; where even the stars were unfamiliar.

The hair on the back of his neck and on his forearms rose as sudden sounds filled the air, the sounds of many voices speaking at once, rising and rising in volume like a successful party. Will swiveled his head, his eyes wide and dry in the black-and-silver night.

Abruptly the noises changed to howls, overlapping cascades of howls, and Will realized it must be coyotes. They sounded just like every kid's coyote imitation he'd ever heard, but he never knew about the yapping voice-sounds before. Was that normal for coyotes? Or did it have something to do with him, his presence in their world? Were they talking about him?

The howling went on and on until Will longed for the enormous quiet that had unnerved him only a few minutes before. The howling now appeared to be localized at the base of some rocky cliffs rising sharply about half a mile behind Sam Webb's trailer. The cliffs were in deep moon-shadow, but Will could imagine hundreds of coyotes congregated there, planning to chase him down and add his bones to those probably bleaching elsewhere on the sand.

He started walking, fast, eyes wide, looking around as he hurried. In the warmth of the night, his forehead was beaded with sweat and he could feel drops sliding between his shoulder blades.

As abruptly as the coyotes had begun, they stopped, and the stillness was ear-splitting. Had they decided to charge, or whatever coyotes did?

He wasn't going to wait to find out. He sprinted the mile or more to the trailer in back of the Snakebite, and when he slammed the door safely behind him, his heart was pounding so hard he expected to see the front of his T-shirt lifting. If the coyotes didn't get him, a heart attack might.

He was standing at the kitchen sink downing his third glass of water when he heard the car crunch over the sand behind the trailer, and the engine stop.

Paige flipped her keys onto the couch and came into the kitchen. "What happened to you?" she asked. "You're soaking."

"I've been running. Did you know it's full of coyotes out there?"

"Oh, sure. They can be pretty noisy, but I never hear them when the air-conditioning's on. Sounds like they're having a party when they get started."

"You mean that's a normal sound?" He began filling the sink with hot water. "I thought they were hatching a plan to get me."

"This *is* their place more than it's ours. The animals and the spirits belong here more than we do." She leaned against the refrigerator.

Will turned off the water and put his hands into the sink. "What spirits?"

"The Indians who used to live here. That's why this is such a sacred place to be. They worshipped everything here."

"They must have been hard up for things to worship," he said, swishing his hands around. "There isn't much here."

"You just don't know what to look for. If it's not big and loud and all over you, like your beloved ocean, you don't even see it. You need to learn about subtleties."

She was wrong. He'd noticed the stars and silence and dryness already. And coyotes.

"Since when has subtlety been your strong point?" he countered. "You could step over a pile of dirty clothes the size of Rhode Island without noticing it."

"That's not what I'm talking about."

"Well, what are you talking about?"

She snatched open the refrigerator, grabbed a Diet Coke, and slammed the door shut. "I don't know why I bother. I think you go out of your way to misunderstand me."

"What have I misunderstood?" he said to her back as she crossed the living room and shut herself into her bedroom.

He pulled the plug and dried his hands. Every female out here is furious or weird or both, he thought. And the only man I've met is nursing some mysterious big wound. And the off-roaders are thrill-seekers with a death wish. Am I the last rational being in this part of the world?

6

There was a line of off-roaders waiting for breakfast in front of the Snakebite at six-thirty Sunday morning, and things got busier from there.

Will had no time to talk to Paige about anything that wasn't strictly business, nor did he want to.

Mike came in during the worst of the breakfast rush, took one look, and left. Truline happily and obliviously monopolized a stool at the counter, drinking her weak tea and passing out *Let Not Your Heart Be Troubled* buttons to anybody bold enough to ask her if she was almost finished. No sign of Sam, who was apparently smart enough to fix his own breakfast on Sunday.

There was a slack period of about eight minutes between the last of the breakfasters and the first lunchers, but by then Will had fallen into a rhythm of constant motion, with every movement purposeful. He felt like an oiled machine, moving smoothly from flipping burgers and frying chicken patties to slicing tomatoes and ladling out chili. He was getting a pretty inflated idea of himself when he stuck a cup of ice cream, milk, and frozen strawberries under the milk-shake machine and, for reasons that remained forever hidden from him, the mixture exploded out of the cup to hit him, the ceiling, and every accessible surface behind the counter.

He stood, dripping and holding the empty cup, as the entire population of the Snakebite broke into applause, hoots, and whistles. Will was glad the milk shake was strawberry. Having it all over his face disguised the fact that he was the same color underneath.

There was nothing to do but stop cooking long enough to clean things up sufficiently to continue. He'd be more thorough after they closed. For now, scraping cooked milk shake off the grill took precedence over washing the ceiling. And, watching Paige step daintily over a pink puddle on the floor, he knew he'd be the one to do it.

Washing the ceiling after closing was what he was doing when Mike's voice interrupted him. "I hear you were the entertainment this afternoon."

He looked down at her from the top step of the ladder. "How did you get in here?"

"The back door was open."

He wrung the sponge out as hard as he could. "Paige was supposed to lock up when she left."

"How come she's not helping you clean up?"

"She had a headache and went to lie down. Besides, she said it was my mess."

Mike picked at a spot of dried milk shake on the counter. "Could you . . . use some help?"

Will almost fell off the ladder. "Look at this place. What do you think?" He wasn't sure if she was offering or setting him up for one of her insults.

"Have you got another sponge and bucket?"

He looked down at her. She'd spoken so softly he could hardly hear her. He shrugged. "Under the sink."

Without a word, she filled the bucket and went to work

on the milk-shake spots on the counter, floor, napkin dispensers, and assorted other café parts.

By the time Will finished washing the ceiling, the wall, and the numerous crevices of the milk-shake machine, Mike was finished, too. They each had a bucket of scummy pink suds and hands about the same color.

"We've got matching dishpan hands," Mike said as they emptied their buckets into the sink.

"Thanks for helping," Will said. He put his bucket under the sink, took hers, and stacked it with his. "Why did you?"

She turned her back, rummaging on shelves until she found a bottle of hand lotion. Her narrow shoulders went up and then down. "Temporary insanity?" She rubbed her hands together. "Want some lotion?"

"Sure."

She handed him the bottle. "Will you be going to school tomorrow? Or is this your new career choice?" The edge was back in her voice.

"I'll be going to school," he said carefully.

"Until you came, I was the only one from this side of the valley who went to the high school. So my mother got me a car. If you want a ride . . . well, I go by here at seven forty-five every morning." She stood by the back door. "If you're out front, I'll stop." The screen door slammed behind her.

Will was waiting by the road in front of the Snakebite at seven-thirty just in case she was early. She wasn't. At precisely seven forty-five, an old orange VW came down the empty road and stopped next to him.

He heard the music before he opened the car door,

and once the door was open, it was so loud it almost knocked him over. "Isn't that kind of loud?" he asked.

"I like it loud," she yelled. "I added a couple of speakers in the back so it's even more wrap-around."

"What is it?"

"Mozart. *Eine kleine Nachtmusik.* Can you believe he heard all this in his head and wrote down just what he heard, with almost no revising?"

"What?"

"Never mind."

They drove the rest of the way to school without speaking, though there were a lot of questions Will wanted to ask. It would be just like her, he thought, to have the music too loud on purpose, so she wouldn't have to talk to him. Wouldn't she know he'd be apprehensive? Didn't she remember how she felt when she first came here? Or maybe he was wrong. Maybe other people loved changing schools in their senior year and he was just some kind of wimp to mind.

For miles they passed nothing but sand and scrubby desert plants before they whizzed past the scattered homes and few stores of Anza to the high school on the other side of town.

Mike whipped the car into a parking spot and turned off the stereo. "I'll be here at lunchtime if you want to join me," she said, grabbing a black bag from the back seat and walking away from him. Today she wore baggy black shorts and the same black T-shirt—or maybe an identical one—she'd worn all weekend. The black bag hung on her shoulder and looked heavy enough to bring her to her knees, but she trudged determinedly away.

He shook his head, locked the car doors, and went to the office to get registered.

The school was small, a one-story structure of fifties design, with a sandy track and a fancy new swimming pool behind it. A graphic of something—arrows? waves?—had been painted across the front in turquoise and gave it a trendy look, like an old lady in a miniskirt. The front of the school was landscaped in sand and cactus, with sagebrush and creosote bushes hedging in at the edges of the cleared areas. The bushes were as high as Will's head, and from what he could see, there probably wasn't anything worth mentioning beyond them.

By the middle of first period, Will had been registered, given a schedule, issued books, and shown to his first class. When he entered, the teacher stopped talking and every head turned in his direction. He felt the way he had when the strawberry milk shake hit the ceiling.

Even after he'd given the teacher his admit slip and found a seat, he felt as if he were outlined in neon. Heads kept turning to look at him, while he tried to figure out what the teacher was talking about.

When the bell rang, he bolted to the hall before he realized he didn't know which way to go. A blond girl wearing a white ruffled dress and a white bow in her hair came up to him and said, "Need some help?" He recognized her from the class.

"American History? Room 111?"

"I'm going there, too." He walked beside her. "All seniors have to take it, so you're either in second period or fifth period with Mr. Lukkens."

"Oh."

"Where'd you move from?"

"Imperial Beach. I'm Will, by the way. Will Griffin."

"Hi. I'm Cindy Naughton."

"Hi."

They arrived at the door of room 111 just behind Mike, who gave them a black scowl and lugged her book bag to her seat.

Mr. Lukkens was a slow, careful, soporific lecturer who spent the hour talking in a monotone about the Continental Congress. Around him, Will could see people dozing, doodling, doing math homework. Cindy filed her nails, and Mike wrote furiously in a notebook. He took a few notes at first and then quit when he realized Mr. Lukkens was reading from the textbook.

Cindy leapt to his side as soon as the bell rang. "Where to next?" she asked.

As Will dug in his pocket for his schedule, he was jolted heavily from behind.

"Excuse me," Mike said loudly. "You're blocking the door." She pushed him aside, shoving him into Cindy. His annoyance with Mike was tempered by Cindy's warm, soft, yielding front pressed against him.

"Geez, I'm sorry," he said, feeling himself once again become the color of a strawberry milk shake.

"No problem," Cindy said, and unless he was mistaken, she leaned into him, giving him one last firm impression of her convexity before they parted. "That girl Mike always acts so obnoxious," she said.

"Yeah?" He was so distracted, all he could think to do was pull his schedule from his pocket and show it to her.

"You've got Contemporary Moral Problems next," she said.

I may indeed, he thought. "What room?"

"I'll show you." As they walked down the hall together, she asked, "What did you think of Lukkens?"

"Tedious. I'm glad I don't have him after lunch. I could barely stay awake as it was."

"As long as you read the chapters, you can do whatever you want in class. Are you going to go out for basketball?"

"I hadn't thought of it. I'm more of a swimmer. Is there a swim team here?"

"Not until the spring. You're so tall, I thought of basketball."

"I don't know. I've never liked it."

"Well, I'll think of something good for you to do. Here's your class. See you later." She twiddled her fingers at him and went off down the hall.

Being taken over by a cute blonde was certainly something that didn't happen to Will every day, and he found himself assaulted by conflicting emotions as he found a chair in Contemporary Moral Problems: pleasure, apprehension, and performance anxiety.

Cindy was waiting to take him to his next class, and again at lunchtime. He had a fleeting thought of Mike eating her lunch in the old orange VW, but he hadn't made her any promises. Having lunch with Cindy would probably be a lot more fun than sitting in a hot car with somebody who'd never heard of smiling.

After school, Cindy walked with Will to the parking lot, where she got into her shiny blue Honda. "See you tomorrow," she called, backing out of her parking space.

Mike sat waiting in the VW, the music louder, if possible, than it had been that morning. As soon as he shut the door, she ejected the tape and started the car. "I waited for you at lunch."

"Sorry. I had lunch in the arbor. I didn't think you were counting on me."

"I wasn't," she snapped. "Though why you'd want to eat, never mind anything else, with someone as vapid and jejune as Cindy Naughton, I can't imagine."

"Vapid? Jejune? Are these English words? Anyway, what do you care who I eat lunch with?"

"You can do anything you want, anywhere you want, with anyone you want. But Cindy? I thought you were more discriminating."

"What are you talking about? All I did was eat lunch with somebody who was *nice* to me, a concept apparently unknown to you. And what do you know about what I like?"

Mike had the accelerator floored and the VW flew, rattling and clanking alarmingly, down the straight empty road to Agua Seca.

"I thought I was a pretty good judge of character," she said. "I thought you and I might have something in common."

"Whatever could that be? Why would you think so? We've hardly exchanged a civil word since we met."

"Never mind. I don't want to talk about it." She shoved the tape into the cassette player and Mozart burst into flower around them, drowning speech and, almost, thought.

Mike didn't turn the music off when she stopped in front of the Snakebite. When Will got out of the car, he yelled, "Same time tomorrow?"

She reached for the door handle, slammed the door, and roared off without a word.

"Does that mean yes or no?" he shouted after her. Then he shrugged and went around to the back door of the café, which had a CLOSED sign in the front window.

Truline sat at the counter, drinking tea with Paige.

"Hi, Willie," Truline said, as he dumped his books on the end of the counter and poured himself a glass of milk. He would have liked a milk shake, but he was still leery of the machine. "How was school?"

"Okay."

Paige didn't even look at him. He knew her. She wasn't going to offer him any chance to complain about his situation.

"Just okay?" Truline asked. "You can be a light that shines for others, you know. Then you reap rewards for yourself."

"Is your real name Truline?" Will asked.

She laughed. "So many people ask me that. It's as real a name as I'll ever have. It's the name the Lord gave me when I was saved. I heard His voice just as clear as I hear yours, saying to me, 'Ruby Jean, you're mine now and I'm calling you Truline.' I like it lots better than Ruby Jean."

"It's different," Will said, finishing his milk. "I guess I'll go do my homework."

"Can I give you a *Let Not Your Heart Be Troubled* button?"

"No, thanks. You gave me one yesterday." On his way out, before he let the back door slam, he said, "Hi, Paige." Then he went on to the trailer.

7

The next morning, he was at the roadside again at seven-thirty. If Mike drove right by him, he'd still have time to take Paige's car.

At seven forty-five the VW came flying up the road, and just when he was sure she wasn't going to stop, she slammed on the brakes and, to terrible screeching and shuddering, the car stopped about ten feet past him.

That's how it went for the rest of the week. Every morning, Mike looked as if she was going to drive right by him, then came to a violent stop and drove him to school with Mozart—he supposed it was Mozart—on loud enough to make his head ring.

Every day, he had lunch with Cindy, and as he ate his ham-and-cheese sandwich, he wondered what Mike was eating out in the parking lot. The drive home was as empty of conversation and as full of violins and French horns as the morning ride had been.

With relief, Will got out of the car on Friday afternoon, hoping Mike would boycott the Snakebite for the weekend and he wouldn't have to see her again until Monday. She'd worn black all week, with strange big jangling earrings, and hadn't said one word to him since Monday afternoon.

He had to go right to work, getting things ready for

the dinner business that would start up as off-roaders began arriving for the weekend.

"Hey, Paige," he said as he patted out hamburgers. "What have you been doing all week? I've hardly seen you."

"Oh, this and that. Reading, hiking, exploring, thinking about buying a dune buggy."

"You've got to be kidding. We can't afford that."

"I wouldn't have to pay for it all at once."

"Come on, Paige. We've got to save some money. Anyway, we've already got a car."

"Will." He could hear her forcing patience into her voice. "You have to think of the here and now. All we have is the present moment. Why not enjoy it to the hilt? This place cries out for a dune buggy. Think of what you can see and do with one. It would be an education in itself."

"Paige," he said in despair, "don't you ever think about the future? It *will* arrive. It's not a crime to think about it. You have to do *some* planning."

"Planning's for old men. Youth is the time for spontaneity."

He'd never heard Paige use that word before, though her life was living proof that she knew what it meant. He'd put money on the idea that Timothy had used that word recently to Paige.

"Your vocabulary's sure improved since you got interested in"—he hesitated—"the desert."

"You object to that? You're always telling me I need to improve myself. Now you want to criticize me when I do? Or can I only do it to your specifications?"

He squeezed a hamburger patty until it came between

his fingers, like mortar between bricks. Talking to Paige was like throwing words out the window. "It's not your vocabulary that makes it hard for me to understand you."

"Then maybe you're the one with the problem, not me."

Six laughing men in baseball caps and T-shirts, all bearing slogans advertising different products, came in the door and took a table. "Bring us six of your coldest beers, beautiful," one of them called to Paige, "and put a fast chill on six more."

Paige threw Will a hard look and opened the cooler for the beers.

When the Snakebite closed at eight, there were still two tables of diners finishing their meals, and Will was wild to get out of there and go do something. Anything. He cleaned up as he waited for the tables to finish, and mixed pancake batter for the morning. As he wiped down the hood over the grill, he thought of Sam Webb and his wood carvings. Will's fingers curved around the sponge he held and he remembered his pleasure in shaping the piece of beeswax with the short sharp knife. That's what he wanted to do: go see Sam. He wanted to be with somebody who, even though he had a mysterious past, knew how to have a normal conversation, unlike Paige or Mike or Truline; someone who didn't make him feel conspicuous and self-conscious, the way Cindy did, with her warm blue-eyed gaze; someone who didn't want anything from him, the way the Snakebite's customers did; someone who didn't baffle him the way Paige did, and Mike, too.

By the time the last person went out the door, Paige

was ready to go too, and all Will had to do was mop the floor. Paige had promised to come in early the next morning and clean the bathrooms. When he got to the trailer, she'd already changed into a clean shirt and a fresh pair of jeans and had the car keys in her hand.

"Where are you going?" he asked.

"To Manzanita to listen to some music at a place over there. The Prickly Pear."

"Who with?"

"Timothy. See you in the morning." She sounded belligerent and defensive, but he was too tired to do more than nod.

"Early. Don't forget those bathrooms," he said as she walked away from him.

He'd changed clothes before it occurred to him that Sam Webb might have something else to do that night. He picked up the phone book, thinner than a paperback Western, and looked for his number.

"Hi, Sam. It's Will Griffin."

"Hi, Will. You ready for another whittling lesson yet?"

"How's tonight?"

"Anytime. I'll put the Cokes and the beeswax on ice."

Will liked the idea of someone waiting for him, making ready for him. He imagined Sam moving around his neat rooms, making the small preparations for Will's arrival: lighting lamps, looking in the refrigerator, thinking about what to teach him. It gave him a good feeling.

The desert was quiet as Will walked to Sam's: no yipping or howling, only an occasional dry rustle in the bushes by the road—the small nocturnal creatures coming out of hiding. Light from a gibbous moon flooded his way and he felt none of the fear of his last walk this way.

A pumpkin sat on Sam's top step, its face artfully carved into a skeptical expression, with arched eyebrows and a twist to its mouth. It looked something like Sam.

"How do you like my self-portrait?" Sam asked, opening the door to Will's knock.

"It's great. Having your whittling knives must make it easier. All I can ever do with a kitchen knife is triangles."

"By next Halloween, they'll be putting your jack-o'-lanterns in museums."

"Probably," Will said, laughing. "I forgot it was Halloween."

"You've had a lot to think about. It's a night for little kids anyway, and there's none of them around here. Kids and restless spirits."

"Paige says the desert's full of restless spirits." He took the chair he'd sat in the last time he'd been there.

"Empty places always make people think that. Don't know why. If I was a spirit, I'd be a lot more restless in Los Angeles. It's a sight easier to get comfortable here than it is there."

"Not for everybody."

"Well, fortunately, not everybody's meant to live in a city. You and your sister, you're the most restless spirits I've seen in a while."

"What about your friend Mike? She's more restless just standing still than anybody I ever saw, except maybe Paige."

"Well, Mike's a seeker, looking for her spot. I think she's making progress. What about Paige?"

"Who knows? I'm not sure Paige has a spot."

"Not everybody does. But most do. There's a writer named Durrell who says there's a home landscape locked in every soul—the place you think of when you think of home. That's so for me. The desert's my home landscape."

"Near the ocean's mine. Do you really think that's true, about the home landscape?"

"As true as most things. There's some that are wanderers in their souls. Maybe that's Paige. And there's some that just ain't particular. But me, I like the desert." As he went to the kitchen for their drinks, he said, "Now tell me about school. What was the best part and what was the worst?"

"The best part," Will mused, thinking aloud. "I guess it's that I'm a little ahead from my last school. I won't have to work too hard. And this girl, Cindy, who keeps hanging around me. She makes it interesting." He wasn't sure why, but he felt uncomfortable talking about Cindy. "The worst part is car-pooling with Mike. She keeps the stereo on so loud in her car I'm going to have to get some earplugs. And she acts like she hates me. It's really depressing to ride with her. I can't figure out why she even offered."

"It was her idea?"

"Yeah. Sunday she came to the Snakebite and volunteered to help me clean up a mess I'd made. I almost fell off my ladder. Then she offered to drive me to school. Now she won't talk to me. Is she certifiable, or what?"

"Did Cindy start hanging around you, by any chance, between the time Mike was being nice to you and the time she stopped talking to you?"

"Well, yeah. But why should that bother Mike?"

"Mike's a lonely, complicated girl. She might have seen something in you, something that escapes an old guy like me," he said, lifting one eyebrow, so that he looked like his pumpkin, "that caused her to do some hoping. Then along comes Cindy."

"Mike? Be serious. She's got all the charm and appeal of a tarantula."

"The tarantulas around here have painful bites, but they only bite when they're afraid, and they're not poisonous."

"You really think she . . . I mean, finds me . . . you know . . ."

"Such modesty," Sam said, taking a swallow of beer. "Surely a big galoot like you has had girls interested in him before."

"Actually, no. They kind of scare me, you know, and besides, I had an after-school job and Paige and my mom to worry about." He looked down at the glass in his hand. "Mostly, I guess, I'm chicken."

"You're just waiting to grow into your feelings. I was that way, too. But my guess is you're about there, and that can be a strange place, too."

"Yeah." Suddenly there was a lot Will wanted to ask Sam—things about girls and growing up and being a man—but he didn't know how to. He'd never had a grown man to talk to before, not like this, just sitting around having a drink and an easy conversation.

"You might as well tell me what Cindy's like," Sam said. "She seems to have impressed you."

Will made an amused, embarrassed sound. "Sometimes I think that's what she's trying to do, the way she's always leaning on me."

"Oh, one of those. You better watch out, boy. She's got some serious designs on you."

"How can you tell?"

"The ones who make physical contact early are in a hurry to get something started."

"Yeah? What kind of something?" He looked at the battered toes of his high-top sneakers so he wouldn't have to look at Sam. This was what he wanted to talk about, but he was afraid he'd seem like a dope.

"Any kind of something. Whatever they can get going, but the quicker and the more exclusive, the better. These are people who need to be attached to a person of the opposite sex and who aren't satisfied until they've done that. I'm about positive that's where you're headed with Cindy. Is that where you want to be headed?"

Will continued to study his sneakers. He wasn't sure he wanted to be headed anywhere with Cindy. He couldn't deny that he liked being pursued by her, though he had to admit he also felt the way he had the night he'd heard the coyotes. Neither could he deny that he liked the way she felt when she leaned against him. But he'd only seen her for the first time four days ago. He didn't know anything about her. It was strange, now that he thought about it, but he felt he knew more about Mike than he did about Cindy, even though he hadn't spoken to her in days.

"Guess that's a harder question than I figured," Sam said.

Will was tempted to make it into a joke, to say something that deflected Sam's interest, and why he didn't, he was never quite sure. Maybe he was tired of joking over his feelings, the way he always had with Jay.

"It is a hard question," Will admitted. "I like the way she wants to be with me. It's flattering, and that's hard to resist. But she makes me nervous, too. She crowds me, you know? She's always around. And I know she's expecting something from me, I can feel her *wanting*, but I don't know what she wants. I don't want to feel like I *have* to give it to her. Does this make any sense?"

"Makes plenty of sense. This might be a good time for you to back up some from Cindy, till you get to know her better, figure out how you want things to be between you two."

"That sounds right," Will said. "I could do that." A little shyly he added, "Thanks."

"Having somebody to talk things over with can help a fellow figure things out. Small things or big things."

"I'll take your word for it."

"Good," Sam said. "It's high time somebody around this wide spot in the road started treating me like the genius I am."

Will laughed, self-consciously, and finished his Coke. He'd liked talking man to man with Sam, but he was glad that Sam, by his joke, had signaled the end of that kind of conversation.

"You ready for another lesson now?" Sam asked him.

"Yeah." He took his glass into the kitchen and put it in the sink. When he came back to the living room, he said, "I've been thinking all day about how I can make that dog better. Once my hand even twitched as if I were really whittling."

"I think you're a natural, boy," Sam said, turning on the light in the workshop.

"Right. That's why my dog ended up looking like a sand dune last time."

"At least it looked like *something*." Sam handed him a

knife and some wax, took up his own carving, and they sat working in the workshop's hard chairs.

Occasionally Sam would offer a suggestion to Will about the angle at which to hold his knife, or how deep to make his cuts, but mostly they worked in silence. Once Sam went to the kitchen for a soft drink, and he brought another one for Will, too.

"One beer's my limit," he said. "Anyway, it's true what they say about beer—you only rent it. It doesn't stay in you long enough for you to consider it bought."

Will laughed, took the can, and went back to work. His lump of wax was actually starting to look like a dog.

After a time—Will didn't know how long—Sam stood, stretched, and said, "That's enough. You better stop now if you want to be able to use that hand tomorrow."

Will felt as if he were coming out of a coma. He flexed his hand and was amazed at how sore and stiff it was. While he'd been working, he hadn't noticed it at all.

"What time is it?"

"Almost midnight. You planning on doing any sleeping tonight?"

"Not much, I guess. But look at this." He extended his wax dog. "What do you think?"

Sam took the figure and examined it slowly. "You learn fast, boy."

"You think so? I didn't know what I was doing, but I just kept doing it."

"You've got the right idea. That's how a lot of living gets done, too."

"It looks like a dog this time, right?"

"It looks like a dog," Sam agreed. "Next time you can do it in wood."

"Really? You think I'm ready for wood?"

"Give it a try. The wax is here if you want to go back to it."

"Can I come tomorrow night?"

Sam was silent for a moment, and Will rushed in: "Just say no if you want. It's Saturday night. You probably have something else to do."

"Saturday night's the same as any other night to me now. You made me think about another boy I knew once." Again he hesitated. "Sure. Come tomorrow."

Will ducked his head to hide the pleasure he was sure his face must show. He felt shy about showing how happy he was that Sam would let him come again. Who had the other boy been, he wondered. Someone Sam didn't want to remember?

He pulled on his windbreaker as he went out the front door. The night was cool, and so dark the stars seemed to tremble in the sky. Once again the silence enveloped him until he thought he should be able to feel it—something heavy, soft, and smooth. He wondered if his ears were turning, the way a cat's did, searching for a sound.

Paige was still out when he got home and he had a feeling he knew who would be cleaning the bathrooms the next day.

8

He was right. He even had to run back to the trailer twice after he'd opened the Snakebite, but, fortunately, before any customers arrived, to make sure Paige was dressed and on her feet.

She stumbled through the morning, delivering breakfasts to the wrong tables, and once dropping a whole tray of dirty dishes on the floor. They hit so hard the contents of a pitcher of pancake syrup shot straight to the ceiling and dripped back down on her. Will knew he'd be the one up on the ladder later, and wondered why they couldn't seem to spill things simply, on the floor.

During the late-morning lull, while Paige sat on a stool at the counter, her head down on her crossed arms, Will washed the ceiling.

"What's wrong with you?" he asked. "Are you sick?"

She shook her head, rolling it against her arms.

"You can't stay out so late and still get to work at six," he said, knowing he was wasting his breath, and deciding not to mention that he had stayed out late and managed to get to work on time.

She stood up. "I'm going to get an aspirin." She went out the back door.

Will gave the ceiling a final wipe and dropped the sponge in the bucket.

The bell on the door tinkled as he came down the ladder, and he looked over his shoulder to see Mike come in and take a seat at the counter. "Milk shake?" she said.

"Syrup. Don't ask." Then he was sorry he'd said it. The first words she'd spoken to him in almost a week, and he'd shut her up.

"Paige have anything to do with it? I saw her last night at the Prickly Pear. I'd hazard a guess she wasn't feeling too steady at 6 a.m."

"She'll be okay. She's just tired."

"I bet."

He emptied the bucket and put the ladder back in the storeroom, so furious he had to stand in the dark, among the gallon cans of catsup and chili, and clench his fists. As angry as he got at Paige's behavior, he got angrier still at anybody who criticized her. That was his privilege only.

He heard the sound of a cup banging on the counter and that caused another tide of anger to rise in him. She had some nerve! He hurtled out of the storeroom, only to find that the cup was being banged by a man with a cigarette box tucked up into his T-shirt sleeve and a tattoo of an eagle showing on his shoulder.

"Hey, man. Two cheeseburgers to go, okay, and onion rings. Couple six-packs, any kind, and can you fill up my thermos with coffee?"

"Right," Will said, taking the thermos. Mike sat at the counter, demurely reading the menu. He threw burgers on the grill, stuck a couple of six-packs in a plastic bag, filled the thermos, and started the onion rings. It always amazed him how efficient he could be even when his mind was whirring away on something unrelated to what he was doing.

What a jerk he was. He knew it wasn't fair or logical to be angry at Mike for what she'd said when he was really angry at Paige. Why couldn't she be dependable? Why did he always have to take up her slack? Why couldn't he get her to change?

He drained the onion rings, wrapped the cheeseburgers and stuck them in a sack, added the onions. He didn't care if Paige became a nun, just so long as she found whatever it was she was looking for, so he could quit worrying about her.

He handed the tattooed man the bag and put his money in the cash register. He was still staring at the digital numbers when the bell tinkled, signaling the man's departure, and Mike cleared her throat. He looked up at her.

"What do you want?" he asked.

"I guess I asked for that. I'm sorry."

He blinked. Sam was right when he called her complicated. He wondered if schizophrenic might not be a better word.

"What's with you, anyway? You change moods faster than I can follow. You don't talk to me for a week for reasons unknown to the rational mind, then you come in here, insulting my sister and apologizing. I don't get it."

"Insulting your sister? All I said was I saw her at the Prickly Pear last night and that she was probably tired this morning. I'd say you're a bit too sensitive where she's concerned. How come?"

"None of your business. Where do you get off, asking me something like that? How come you didn't talk to me all week? That's more to the point."

She looked around. "I guess we should talk about that," she said in a reasonable tone. "But not now. You'll be swamped with lunch people in a few minutes."

"Okay, when?" He wanted to get this straight with her.

"Tonight, after closing? I can come by."

"Fine." He turned away to slice more tomatoes for the lunchtime hamburgers, and when he looked around, she was gone. How she got out without making the bell on the door jingle, he couldn't figure.

Paige, with fresh eye makeup and a look of resolve, came back just as he was getting too busy to handle everything by himself. She was quiet and efficient for the rest of the day and he left her alone.

"You go on," she told him at seven forty-five. "I'll clean up and close. You've worked extra for me today."

"But the place is still full."

"They've got their food. All I have to do is bring more coffee and take their money. I'm going to put the CLOSED sign up. This has been a long enough day already."

"Okay. I won't argue. If, uh, anybody comes in asking for me, I'll be in the trailer."

Paige just looked at him and nodded.

9

He'd showered and changed already when he heard the knock at the door. Mike stood on the top step, looking as normal as he'd ever seen her. Her hair was pulled back neatly and she had pearls in her ears instead of her usual big ugly earrings. She wore a clean pink T-shirt under white overalls that actually seemed to fit her. She looked contrite and twelve years old.

"Hi," he said.

"Hi." She looked off over his shoulder. "You want to take a walk while we talk? I love the desert at night, even if I hate it the rest of the time."

"Okay. But it's getting cool. Don't you have a jacket?"

"I forgot mine. When it's hot in the daytime, I forget about the nights."

That sounded like something Paige would say. He figured Mike's fluctuating moods should stir up enough heat to keep her warm.

"You can borrow a sweater, I guess." He left her standing by the open door while he got his windbreaker and his tan pullover for her.

"Thanks." She tied the sweater around her neck by the sleeves, and it hung almost to her thighs.

"Where do you walk around here at night?" Will asked.

"Anywhere. What difference does it make?"

"Aren't you afraid?"

"Of what? The coyotes are noisy, but they're not after me. The snakes are in their holes. Most animals out here are shy and cautious, anyway. They run when they hear you coming and don't hurt anybody unless they're trapped or scared."

They walked for a while in silence.

"I've never heard quiet like this," Will finally said. This walk was her idea. There was supposed to be talk that went with it, but he seemed to be the only one who remembered that.

"You can hear it, can't you?" she said. "I thought you'd be someone who could. That's what made me so mad. Cindy doesn't hear quiet. She just wants to fill it up with noise. There are people who can listen to silence and there are those who can't."

That seemed an odd thing for someone with extra speakers in her car to say, but he didn't want to get sidetracked.

"You stopped talking to me because you think Cindy doesn't like silence? Are you serious?" But even as he said it, he knew what she meant. He felt the same way when Paige refused to understand how he felt about the sight and sound and smell of the sea. Some people understood and some didn't and that's all there was to it.

"Yes, I'm serious. Too serious, probably." She sounded as if she were talking to herself. "But that's how I am. It's hard to find people like me. Even if I didn't have to move around so much with my mother, I still don't think I'd have many friends. I'm not easy to know and I . . ."

She stopped. "Am I going to feel stupid for telling you this stuff?"

He stuck his hands in his pockets. "I don't know. You haven't told me much yet."

"You tell me something. About you. So I won't feel like this is so one-sided."

What was she talking about? He thought she was going to explain why she hadn't spoken to him all week, and now he felt in over his head somehow.

It was easier for him to think standing still, so he stopped walking. "Mike, I'm trying to be cooperative here, but I don't know what's going on. I thought you were going to tell me what made you so mad at me."

"That's what I'm doing, you mental defective."

"Hold it. Mental defective? No wonder you don't have many friends." They stood in the center of the straight, dark road, facing each other. She cast a small shadow in the moonlight, but her anger made her seem bigger on the inside than on the outside. "I've got a feeling this doesn't have much to do with me. Who are you so mad at?"

"See! Not everybody could figure that out." She still sounded furious. "I thought we could understand each other. But instead you go off with that . . . that bimbo . . ."

"Now wait a minute—"

"Well, she is. One of the reasons she was so glad to see you is because she's gone out with just about every boy in school already, plus the one who works at the gas station. She doesn't know anything about being a friend. All she knows how to be is—do you know what they call her at school? The Egg."

"Because she's hard-boiled?"

"Because she goes over easy." She turned her back on him. "I could be a real friend to you."

How did he get himself in this spot? What was he supposed to do now? He wished Sam was there to ask.

"I hesitate to mention this, but you haven't acted very friendly."

"I helped you clean up the milk shake. I drove you to school."

"But you're always so mad. How did I know that's how you act when you're being friendly?"

With a start, Will realized he was enjoying this, standing in the desert yelling at this odd, angry girl and having her yell at him. For all the yelling he and Paige did at each other, he never had the feeling she really wanted to understand what he was saying; she was always so busy listening to herself.

He took Mike's hand and pulled her to the side of the road. "No use getting run over just when the fight is going so well." Yellow pinpoints grew into headlights as a car tore down the road past them. The noise of its motor seemed unnaturally loud in the empty night.

Mike pulled her hand from Will's and stalked along the roadside ahead of him, head down, hugging her elbows and looking like a pouty child.

"Why don't you put on the sweater if you're cold?"

Mike continued to stamp along, the sweater over her shoulders.

"Come on, Mike," he said finally. "Let's finish this."

She turned around. "I'm so tired of being mad. Sometimes it hurts inside too much."

"I know."

"I thought you might."

He didn't want to get into why she thought that. Instead, he asked, "What are you so mad about?"

"Have you got ten years?"

"Just give me a piece of it." He wasn't clear why, but he did want to know.

"Okay. My mother. Out to be a better anthropologist than anybody ever, man or woman, living or dead. And lest anyone think she can't also be a woman, she had a child. Of course, she wouldn't marry the child's father, even though, God knows why, he wanted to. But you can't hire a nursemaid for a husband while you write papers and teach classes and run around the world looking at things with a magnifying glass. Apparently, husbands want more attention than you can get away with giving to dumb little kids. The fact that she's beautiful and charming and smart and talented and intolerant of anybody who's not doesn't make it any better. She regards me as the only project she's ever tackled that didn't turn out the way she wanted. But she keeps trying. I could write a treatise on being a disappointment."

"I don't know how you stop being mad about something like that." He wished he did.

"I don't, either. I think it'll be better once I get away from her, off to college, and start doing things the way *I* want."

"How do you want them?" He walked into the desert from the roadside until he came to a hump of sand, where he sat down. Being out in the big dark night wasn't scary with her along, he realized. Mike sat next to him, untied the sweater, and pulled it on.

"I don't know yet. That's another part of why I'm the

way I am. I lie awake at night thinking 'How do I want to be?' and all I come up with is, 'Out of here.' "

"I can relate to that."

"Doesn't it make you wild, too?"

"Yeah. But what can I do? Paige needs me; we need to stick together, and, for now, she needs to be here. Sure, I get mad at the way she keeps hopping around, but she's doing what you are—trying to figure out what she wants."

"She should know by now."

"Who says? She's only twenty. She's got time." He didn't say she would be twenty-one in two weeks.

"Well, is she making any progress? Do you think what she's looking for is what Timothy's got to offer?"

He shrugged and lay on his back on the sand, his hands behind his head. "I don't know. If it's not, she'll try something else. That's her privilege."

"Am I going to have to try everything there is before I can decide? God, I hope not. I know I love the video camera. I love planning the images, thinking about the story I want to tell. I know I want to go to film school so I can really learn how to do it."

"That's a lot to know. It takes care of the next few years. I'd be happy if I could see that far ahead."

"That's about what to do, not how to be."

"Don't you think doing and being are connected?"

"Does that mean all filmmakers are alike, and all doctors and all teachers?" She sounded angry again. "Being's different."

"But what makes somebody want to be a filmmaker instead of a doctor? Doing has to have something to do with being."

"Doobie, doobie, doo," she sang, and they laughed. She sighed and lay down beside him. "This is getting too Zen for me."

Will looked up at the wide, black, star-studded sky and wondered how important the difference between doing and being really was. Maybe all life, as Sam said, was something you just kept doing, whether you knew how or not.

Mike spoke again. "My mother wants me to film her dig. She thinks she's going to find something great and she wants a record, but you don't need a video camera to take pictures of things that haven't moved in hundreds and thousands of years. And she doesn't want footage of the actual digging because, according to her, it's aesthetically uninteresting. It's such a laugh. She's so organic she won't use an electric mixer because it's too abusive to the food. But she needs a video of inert things. Video is for movement."

"Well, film something moving, then. What moves around here? Anything?"

"Very little. I started filming Sam last fall, when we first got here. He was making those bricks and pouring the foundation."

"What bricks? Foundation for what?"

"He's building a house. An adobe. He made the bricks himself. Eight thousand of them. I helped him a few times. It almost drove me nuts. I'm too impatient. First he had to figure just the right proportions of clay and sand and whatever, so the bricks wouldn't crack. Then he had to make trial bricks until they came out right. I'd have ended up with a house like the careless little pig's—a coyote could blow it down. But not Sam. He fussed over those bricks forever. Then, making them is slow, and they have to dry just right, and be stacked just right, and pass the damp test and the drop test and stuff like that. By then, it was summer and too hot to work."

"When's he going to start again?"

"He has. I'm filming him, but it's so slow. I don't know how he stands it. He's going to do everything: plumbing, wiring, everything. Sometimes I feel like I'm filming Marcella's dig. Sam's a big part of my film, though, and he's a natural teacher, so he makes it interesting, explaining what he's doing."

"You call your mother Marcella?"

"She thinks it's more enlightened. It allows us to relate as autonomous individuals instead of being forced into societally prescribed roles as child and parent. Or something like that. You'd think an anthropologist would know kids need to have parents, even if they are autonomous individuals. I'm still doing all the talking."

"I asked for it."

"Well, you got it," Mike said.

"You know, the stars look different out here. Colder or farther away or something."

"It's you, not them. It's how you're looking at them."

"What do you mean?"

"You feel colder and farther away out here. Farther away from what?"

He didn't know why, but, lying on his back, looking up at those cold stars, it was easy to tell her about the beach and Paige and his mother and father, and even about the black dog. Then they just lay, without speaking. Will felt full in an unfamiliar way: of what he wasn't sure, but he had the tight, slightly uncomfortable feeling of

Thanksgiving dinner—too much of a lot of good things. He would need a while to digest them.

"What time is it?" he asked her, finally.

She sat up and took an old-fashioned pocket watch from her overall pocket. He wasn't surprised. He hadn't expected her to tell time with anything as ordinary as a wristwatch. When she flipped the lid open, a tiny tinkly tune floated into the vast night. "I can't tell. It's too dark."

He sat up, too. "I better go. I told Sam I'd come by after the Snakebite closed. You . . . you want to come, too?"

"No. Well, yes, but I won't. I don't want to louse up the male bonding process."

Will stood up and brushed the sand off the seat of his jeans. "Is that what we're doing? I thought we were having a drink and doing some whittling."

"Men are so simple. Here, let me brush off your back."

Her hands brushed over his shoulders and back and felt good in a way that Cindy's leaning on him never had. He could hardly wait to get to Sam's, where things were, indeed, simpler.

"I was about to give up on you," Sam said, opening the door.

Will crossed to the workshop and picked up his beeswax dog, still on the table. "I was having a talk with Mike."

"A talk? I thought she wasn't doing that." Sam leaned against the doorframe and stroked his mustache.

"You were right. She didn't like Cindy."

"What do you know. So you're friends again?"

"Not again. We weren't to begin with."

"Mike can be a good friend, I think, but a demanding one."

"What do you mean?"

"She'll want a lot from you—a lot of involvement, but a different kind from what Cindy wants. More mental, more emotional. You up for that?"

"I don't know. I'm new at this. How come you know so much?"

"Just living. If you're paying even the slightest bit of attention, you learn a few things. Aside from the ones that hit you right over the head. Course, I'm wrong once in a while, so don't let it prevent you from learning on your own."

"Mike told me you're building a house. You must mean to stay here."

Sam handed him a piece of wood. "This is linden wood. It's soft enough to start on." He picked up his Indian figure. It was finished, but needed polishing, which he began to do with a soft cloth and linseed oil. "I do. This place suits me. Space and silence and few demands. A body can do what he wants. Now, draw your pattern just like you did for the wax."

"Could I come see your house? I've never seen an adobe house being built."

"Not many folks have."

"Why adobe? Why not stay in your trailer?" Will sharpened his pencil and drew the dog.

"A trailer doesn't belong here. It's slapped down on the sand and, sure, you can live in it, but it's always a stranger. Adobe seems to grow out of the land—in a way, it really does, if you make it out of native soil. It blends in, becomes a part. It's beautiful, and fireproof, and soundproof, not that there's much to hear, and good insulation. And cheap to build. I like the idea that my hands'll have been on every inch of my house."

Grinning at Sam's enthusiasm, Will said, "No, really, tell me why."

Sam laughed. "Work on that dog, boy, if you ever want to be a whittler. That's good. You've got the pattern going with the grain of the wood. You're asking for trouble if you try and go across your grain. Besides the fact that it's harder work, you get cracks and splits and a general mess. Anyway, wood's ten times stronger along the grain than across it, because of the vertical nature of wood cells."

After he'd worked for a while, Will said, "Sam?"

"What?"

"Could I come see your house tomorrow after work? We close at three."

"Okay by me. I'll be out there. Mike'll be there, too."

"That's okay. If I'm going to experiment with this friendship idea, I'm going to have to get used to being around her."

10

At the stroke of three on Sunday, Will untied his greasy apron and wadded it into a ball. He threw it into the plastic hamper of Snakebite laundry and had his hand on the back doorknob when Paige grabbed him by a belt loop in the back of his jeans.

"Where do you think you're going? There's an hour of cleanup left here. And I did it last night."

He didn't turn around. "Well, I've got somewhere to go, so I guess you'll be doing it again today. If you're really keeping score, I'm ahead anyway." There were only a couple of hours of daylight left, and he had to see this miracle house of Sam's.

She let go of his belt loop. "What's that supposed to mean?"

"I have to go." He opened the door. "I need to take the car. I won't be back late." He closed the door behind him and whipped his fingers off the knob before he could turn it again; go back inside, and do his job. And probably Paige's, too.

He ran to the trailer, grabbed the car keys from Paige's bureau and a sweater from his room, and jumped in the car.

As he ripped down the highway, following the directions Sam had given him, he let out a breath he hadn't realized he'd been holding. He rolled down the window and yelled out into the bright, empty air.

When he pulled off the narrow road onto Sam's construction site, he saw piles of adobe bricks surrounding a structure of shoulder-high walls. Mike's VW and Sam's pickup were parked in the yard, but no one came out to greet him, and with the motor of Paige's car turned off, there was no sound at all. The closing of the car door, as he got out, seemed loud enough to make him wince.

"Hello?" he said quietly.

"Come on in," Sam called from inside the half-made house.

Will stepped through the frame of the front door and found Sam and Mike sitting on the cool poured concrete of the foundation, their legs straight out in front of them, passing a can of root beer between them. Mike's right hand rested on the top of her video camera as if it were a pet.

"It's the last one," Sam said. "Want a gulp?"

Will shook his head. "I can't stand root beer."

"It's an acquired taste," Mike said.

"Not one I'm interested in acquiring."

Sam's blue work shirt was dark with sweat in great crescents under his arms, and when he stood up and dusted off the seat of his pants, Will saw that the back of his shirt was soaked, too. Mike's hair was pulled away from her face and she'd tied a blue bandana headband-style around her forehead. Beads of perspiration stood out on the bridge of her nose, but the rest of her looked cool and dry.

"Want to stack a few bricks, boy?" Sam asked.

"Sure. How do I do it?"

Sam scooped some mortar from a wheelbarrow with a trowel and smeared it across the top row of bricks to one side of the door. "Like buttering toast," he said. Then he laid bricks on the mortar, wiggling them around a bit to get the fit right, as mortar oozed between them. "That's it. Nothing a dim bulb couldn't do. Just make sure you overlap the bricks by about half, to stagger the grooves between them. Otherwise, the rain'll run straight down the tracks you make. If we ever get any rain. And then point between the layers."

"Point?"

"Scrape out the extra mortar, just use your fingers, so it doesn't weep between the bricks. Some like that weeping look, but not me."

"What are these strings along the wall for?"

"Simple. They're to make sure the wall stays straight up and level. Don't want it wandering off, do I?"

"How much does one of these babies weigh?" Will asked, hefting a brick.

"They're four by ten by fourteen and weigh around thirty pounds," Sam said, spreading more mortar. "Lift a few of them and you'll have biceps the honest way. None of that sissy stuff—lifting weights in some air-conditioned health spa"—the words were rich with ridicule—"surrounded by girls in painted-on outfits."

"Yeah, that sounds terrible," Will said. "Especially the part about the painted-on outfits." He dropped a brick into place as Sam laughed and Mike took a close-up shot of Will's hand adjusting the fit of brick to brick.

Two hours later, with the sun already down behind the mountains, and the shadows long and dark, the three of them secured plastic tarps over the remaining piles of adobe bricks. It was amazing to Will how much progress they'd been able to make when they'd gotten into the rhythm of spreading mortar, laying brick, spreading mortar, laying brick. His shoulders ached from lifting, but, to his disappointment, his biceps looked exactly the same.

"Why do we have to cover these up?" Will asked. "It's not going to rain and you'll be back here tomorrow."

"Sure, that's my plan," Sam said, placing some tools into the back of his pickup, "but you never know. I could take sick tonight and not get back here for a week and a storm could come up in that time. You got to think ahead, boy. Learn to anticipate, not just react to the problem once it shows up. If those bricks got wet, I know how to dry them out, or make new ones, but I don't want to have to do that. I'd rather prevent it in the first place. You two want to have supper with me? I got some chili in the freezer that'll put hair on your chest."

"How could I resist an advertisement like that?" Mike said.

"Me, too," Will said. "Not that I need any more hair on my chest, you understand, he said modestly."

Mike laughed.

All afternoon, the two of them had been careful and polite with each other. Their long conversation last night had been so strange, so unlike anything Will had ever done before, he still wasn't sure what to make of it. He'd had friends, and Jay, of course, but he didn't know much about girls, besides Paige, and he didn't think she counted. And not with any of his friends had he been through the roller coaster of talk that he'd experienced with Mike. She knew more about him now than Paige did; certainly than Jay did. Maybe there was something in the dry, silent space of a desert night that did affect a person's mind; made him say and feel things foreign to his idea of himself. He didn't know if he liked that. It made him feel exposed.

He was glad to be alone in the car as he followed Mike and Sam back to Sam's trailer. It gave him time to decide that he was sorry he'd told Mike so much and sorry he'd listened to her. He didn't want to know about her problems with her mother, or her struggles to decide how to arrange her life. Those were hers, and he didn't want to feel dragged into responsibility for her, any more than he wanted to be dragged into something with Cindy. He had enough on his plate with Paige.

By the time they arrived at Sam's, Will had decided he couldn't stay for dinner. He didn't mind helping Sam with his house—after all, his biceps might benefit—but he didn't want to get mixed up with Mike's problems. If that's what friendship was, he didn't need it.

Sam and Mike stood in the yard waiting for Will to turn off the motor.

Finally Sam came to the window. "We're there."

"Sam, I forgot I told Paige I'd bring the car back early. I have to go home."

"No problem. Mike can follow you and bring you back while I start the chili."

"Oh, I, uh, don't want to inconvenience anybody."

Mike had heard this exchange and slipped back into her car, calling, "Come on. I'll race you to the Snakebite." She started her car, and Sam slapped the side of Will's door and headed for the trailer. Will had no choice but to follow Mike.

On the way back to Sam's, Mike did all the talking. "I

don't think I could stand to live forever way out there in the nowhere the way Sam wants to, but he says the desert's his home landscape. He was in the construction business all his life—did he tell you this already?—but he says the houses he liked best were the ones in the desert. He also says he thinks most people who live this far away from cities are hiding from something. He doesn't seem like he's doing that, but maybe he is. I think people can come here to look for something as well as hide from something. But if you stay too long looking, you may get stuck. I think . . . oh, my God, I almost drove right by Sam's."

Once inside the trailer, Mike went straight to the telephone. Will couldn't avoid overhearing her conversation.

"Marcella, I'm staying at Sam's for dinner . . . Well, I *couldn't* call sooner . . . What difference does it make? . . . You didn't tell me I was supposed to film for you today . . ." Her voice rose in pitch. "Okay, so I forgot. I'll do it tomorrow, or did you dig up the Missing Link already . . . I'm not acting any more hostile than you are . . . All *right*, I'll be home after dinner."

She banged the receiver into its cradle and stood, her hands in the pockets of her baggy shorts, staring at the floor. "It's always such a pleasure transacting business with my mother."

Sam came and put his hand, encased in an oven mitt, on her shoulder. "Ready for a beer?"

"You know I don't drink beer," she said, still looking at the floor.

"I mean a *root* beer. You have your kind while I have my kind."

"Okay." She raised her head and glanced at Will, who sat on the couch, trying to pretend he'd heard nothing. Then she followed Sam into the kitchen, where Will could hear her still.

"I guess I'll go on home. I'm not hungry now, anyway."

"What good's that going to do? Give Marcella a chance to cool down. You, too."

"Marcella never cools down enough to suit me."

"Well, you fan each other's fires, that's for sure." A spoon clanged on the edge of a pan. "Go throw some spoons on the table and I'll serve this stuff up. It's fortifying."

Mike came out of the kitchen with spoons, napkins, and place mats, which she distributed on the round table. She finally met Will's eyes. "See? That's how it always is with her."

"*Were* you supposed to film her dig today?" he asked.

Mike shrugged. "Probably. I don't absorb what she says to me very well."

Sam carried in a tray of steaming bowls. "Come on. Dig in while this is still hot if you want to get a kink in your tail."

Mike pulled out her chair. "I think I've already got one. I want the chest hair. Will can have the kink."

Will sat down, dipped his spoon in the chili, and tasted it. "Yow! I think I'm sprouting hair on the bottoms of my feet. This stuff is great!"

They ate in reverent silence, blowing their noses on napkins, wiping moisture from brows and eyes. When Will's bowl was empty, he leaned back in his chair, belched grandly, and said, "I lift bricks all day, eat fire at night. I am strong like bull."

"And full of bull pucky," Mike said, wiping her running eyes.

"My bull pucky is fine and strong. My shoulders, they ache with the fine ache of man's work under the strong, fine sun. At night I want fire to eat, strong man's drink to drink, and one fine, strong woman to . . ."

"You haven't been reading Hemingway, have you?" Mike interrupted.

". . . to play Parcheesi with," Will finished. "Yeah, I like Hemingway. How could you tell?"

They all laughed, and Will was glad. He was determined to keep the conversation from anything personal. He didn't want to hear any more about what went on between Mike and Marcella Macey.

"I better go now," Mike said, standing up. "I'll be by for you in the morning, Will. You can have a play-by-play of the evening's events at my house."

"Not if Mr. Mozart has anything to do with it." Then he was sorry he'd said that. If she kept the music on in her car, he wouldn't have to listen to the play-by-play.

"Wolfgang does what I tell him to." She picked up her video camera and sighted at them through the viewer. She backed out the door, saying, "This is how the victims looked mere hours before their bodies were found. Chemists are working to identify the substance found in the bowls on the table, but even after intensive analysis, they are far from an answer. More film at eleven." The door closed.

"Want some more?" Sam asked.

"Are you trying to put me in the hospital? I've got to build up some internal calluses before I can do this again."

"You interested in building up some other kinds of

calluses?" Sam leaned toward Will, his elbows on the table.

"What do you mean?"

"You want to help me finish the house? I can only pay you minimum wage, but I could use the help. I'd like to get it roofed by Christmas."

"But I don't know how to do anything."

"Lots of people are out there earning a living who don't know either, boy. I'll show you. Most of it only requires a strong back—like digging the hole for the septic tank, and the leach line trenches, and the trench to the nearest power pole, so I can have underground utilities."

"And all this time I thought you loved me for my mind."

Sam chuckled. "What mind? I know you don't have a lot of free time, but this is a short job."

"Well, sure. I guess so. It'd only be after school, though. I work all weekend, you know. And the days are getting shorter."

"I know. If you want, you could do some indoor things for me, too. I want to carve the door and window lintels, maybe some of the vigas."

"I'm not much of a carver. You know that. And I never heard of a lintel or a viga. What are they?"

Sam pushed away from the table and balanced his chair on its back legs. "A lintel's the beam across the top of a door or window. In an adobe, they're left exposed. A viga's a round ceiling beam that projects through the wall. They're left exposed, too. I want them pretty. I could teach you the simple gouge-and-chisel techniques I need for the designs. It'll be repetitious work."

Will flexed his hands, anticipating the feel of a carving tool in them. "Sure. If you think I can do it."

"I know you can." Sam brought his chair down with a thump. "You want to start something new in the workshop? I'd say your dog's done."

"Okay. I've been thinking about what I'd like to try next. I want to do a coiled rattlesnake. Do you think that's too hard for me?"

"Not at all."

They cleared the table and put the dishes to soak before they went into the workshop. Will liked the way Sam was careful with his things; he kept them clean and put them away and treated them as if he valued them and meant them to last. He knew he'd never find Sam's clothes scattered around his bedroom floor or one of Sam's sandals out on the front walk, or Sam's dirty dishes left for days on the kitchen table.

He also liked the way he felt so comfortable in Sam's workshop, with a knife in his hand and the dark desert outside the windows. If he only had the sound of surf in his ears and some humidity on his skin, he'd be perfectly content—at least until he had to go home to Paige.

11

The next morning, as he waited by the roadside for Mike to pick him up, he hoped she'd have her music on again. As much as he'd hated it last week, he now saw its value. Last week she didn't want to talk to him. This week he didn't want to listen to her. He had enough problems.

The VW rattled to a tidy stop right beside him, and when he opened the door, silence greeted him. "Get in," Mike said.

"Hi."

"Hi. Get in."

"Yeah. Okay." He got in, and the second he shut the door, Mike changed gears and shot off down the road.

"My attorney'll be contacting you about the whiplash," Will said, picking his books up from the floor.

"Maybe I could talk to him about having my mother institutionalized."

"Maybe you could."

"You should have heard her go on last night. You'd think I'd committed a capital crime. She just went on and on and . . . Are you listening?"

"Huh? Yeah, sure. What?"

"My mother."

"Oh, right. She's an anthropologist, right?"

"What's wrong with you? You know she's an anthropologist."

"I guess I just forgot for a minute."

The VW hurtled down the empty road.

"What's going on, Griffin? You getting cold feet?"

"Cold feet about what?"

"Don't you bull pucky me." She hit the steering wheel with the flat of her hand. "And don't you start acting like some ordinary macho jerk who was inoculated against emotions at birth. You talk to me, you hear? I'm not going to let you get away with this chicken-hearted emotional withdrawal. If you and I are going to be friends, we're going to communicate." She drew the word out to about eight syllables at the top of her lungs. "What are you so afraid of?"

"God," he said. "Is this the way you and your mother carry on?"

"So what if it is?" she yelled. "At least we know where we each stand, even if we never agree on anything. Where do you stand? Do you want to be friends or not? And if not, why didn't you say so the other night before I spilled my guts to you, thinking you were interested in what I was saying? Did it give you some kind of sick, hairy-chested thrill to watch me make a fool of myself?"

She seemed to have forgotten he'd told her things, too.

He couldn't help it: he had to admire her fire and her determination to be honest. Playing games with her was impossible: it was truth or nothing.

He recognized her desperation. It was the way he often felt when he argued with Paige. He wanted to shake truth out of her and rarely could. Now he realized how Paige must feel—pinned to the wall. Being forced to say things she didn't want to know, didn't want to admit—so she never said them. Instead, she sulked or disappeared or threw up smoke screens of words; blaming, accusing, evading. But rarely truth.

He knew he had to tell Mike the truth. He didn't want to be like Paige.

"Okay!" he yelled, cutting her off. "I am afraid. I don't know if I can handle friendship with someone as intense as you. I don't know how much you'll want from me and how much I'll want to give." As soon as he said it, he realized she'd forced him to know what he hadn't known before: that he had a choice. He didn't have to give what he didn't want to.

"Well," she said in a calm voice. "Thank you. I knew you could do it."

"Do what?"

"Tell me what you were really thinking. Not some evasive bull pucky, but something real."

"Don't patronize me, Mike." He was trembling with emotion and had to hang tightly onto his books to keep it from showing.

"You're right. You don't do that to a friend. I'm out of practice with friendship. I'm sorry." The apology was matter-of-fact and sincere. Will wasn't sure he'd ever heard one delivered just that way before. "The only way I know to be friends is to be honest. To say what's on my mind as soon as it is on my mind. I'm not afraid to get it back. I might not like it, but I'm not afraid. As far as what you want to give, well, that's something we can talk about. Tell me what you had in mind."

She wheeled the car into the parking lot and turned off the motor.

"I don't know what I had in mind. I thought friendships developed gradually, and you talked about baseball and math class. I have no idea what we're doing here."

"Neither do I. Want to try it?"

"I don't know. You make me nervous."

"I know I do." She looked at her hands on the steering wheel. "I make just about everybody nervous. I can't help it. That's how I am." She squeezed the wheel and sighed. "Okay. Think about it."

"Okay." He got out of the car, hesitated for a moment, looking in at her squeezing the steering wheel, and shut the door. He felt as if he'd done fifteen rounds with the world heavyweight champ; like he'd been cooking at the Snakebite for twenty-four hours without a break. A little undemanding leaning with Cindy sounded very restorative.

She was waiting for him by his locker in a blue dress and bow.

"Hi." He worked the padlock numbers.

She stood close to him. Not quite leaning, but definitely touching. "Hi. Have a nice weekend?"

"Not bad." Not good, either, he thought. "How about you?"

"It was okay. I thought about you."

"You did?" All of a sudden his T-shirt felt too hot and too tight. She was unquestionably leaning now, and it didn't feel as undemanding as he'd thought it would. It was hard putting books into his locker and taking them out, with her doing that, yet he wasn't sure how to discourage her.

"Yeah." It was almost a whisper.

"Huh." He couldn't think of anything to say. At least

with Mike, he could always yell. With Cindy, he was stunned into muteness. What did she want with him, anyhow? Mike left him no doubt. Cindy probably didn't, either. He just couldn't believe it. "We, uh, better get to class."

"Okay." She cuddled her books against her chest while he held his against his thigh, each in their gender-prescribed fashion. As they walked together down the hall, she took his hand and interlaced their fingers, rubbing her thumb across his palm. He swallowed so loudly he thought it must be audible in the principal's office. He was glad Mike wasn't in his first-period class. She'd have a fit if she saw him holding hands with Cindy.

On the way to his second-period class, where he knew he'd see Mike, Will managed to keep juggling books and papers in his arms so that, even though Cindy kept tightly to his side, she couldn't find one of his hands free long enough to grab it. It didn't seem as simple with her as with Mike to choose how close he wanted to be. He couldn't talk to her about it, either, the way he did with Mike.

Mike rolled her eyeballs at him when he entered the classroom with Cindy stuck to him, and he felt a twinge of guilt.

After class, when Cindy went in a different direction from Will, she blew him a kiss and said, "See you in the arbor at lunch."

He had two periods to decide how to respond.

At lunchtime, Will stood in front of his locker, his brown bag in his hand. The arbor with Cindy or the parking lot with Mike? Maybe he should just climb into his locker and shut the door.

The hallway emptied and still Will stood in front of his open locker. Finally he closed the door, twirled the combination lock, and went out the door at the end of the hall, headed for the parking lot.

Mike sat in the driver's seat of the VW, the door open, eating salad out of a plastic bowl in her lap and turning the pages of a book of photographs spread open on the steering wheel. When Will's shadow fell across the pages, she looked up.

"Hi."

"Hi. Mind if I join you?"

She closed the book. "Nope."

He went around to the passenger side and got in. "What are you reading?"

"It's a collection of Margaret Bourke-White's photographs. I'm trying to train my eye."

"Which one? To do what?"

She looked up at him. "Very funny."

"Can you train mine, too?"

"Are you serious? What for?"

He opened his lunch sack and extracted a package of chips and a sandwich. "I'm going to help Sam with the house and do some carving for him. I know how important it is to him, and I don't want to let him down."

"I don't think he'd have asked you if he thought you might let him down. But it wouldn't hurt you to educate yourself."

"You suggesting I'm a dope or something?"

"Don't be so touchy. You asked me to help, remember?"

"Right." He took a big bite from his sandwich and said, with his mouth full, "Talking to you confuses me."

She shrugged.

They ate in silence for a few moments, and then Mike opened the book again. "We might as well start, then. There're several things you need to consider in a photograph's composition. Mass, volume, contrast . . ."

"I have no idea what you're talking about."

"Well, shut up and I'll explain it to you."

Being snapped at by Mike seemed friendlier, at that moment, than being leaned on by Cindy, or working side by side with Paige. He wasn't sorry he hadn't gone to the arbor.

12

Cindy waited for him by his locker the next morning, her mouth arranged in a pout. "I missed you at lunch yesterday. Where were you?"

He twirled the lock. "I had lunch with somebody else."

She ran her hand along his arm. "Who?"

He reached into his locker, pulling his arm away from her. "Mike Macey."

Cindy dropped her hand. "Her? She's so weird. And she's a terrible dresser."

"I didn't notice," he lied.

"Oh, yes. She never wears a dress. And those earrings! She looks like some kind of gypsy or something."

"She's interesting to talk to." He closed his locker.

"Well, today you have to have lunch with me. No excuses. I have something to ask you."

"What?"

"Not until lunch." She gave him a coquettish sidelong look and walked close to him down the hall. He managed to keep his hands out of her reach.

At noon Will returned to his locker to get his lunch. He saw Mike wave to him from the end of the hall just as Cindy came swooping down on him from the other direction. She hooked her arm through his, cast a smug look over her shoulder at Mike, and pulled him toward the arbor. Will looked back, but Mike was gone. "Hey!" he said. "Let go."

"Now, none of that. I told you I wanted to ask you something."

"So ask me. Why do you have to be so mysterious?"

"I'm having a party Saturday night. It's my birthday and I want you to come."

He wasn't sure why, but he'd expected something worse. It was just a party. No big deal. "I work Saturday night. I don't get off till late."

"That's okay. You can come any time you want. I'll be there," she said brightly.

"I guess that'll be okay."

"Great." She hugged his arm against her chest and Will felt hot all over. "You don't have to get me anything too fancy. It's not as if we've been going together for a long time."

It's not as if we're going together at all, he thought. He slipped his arm out of hers. "Excuse me." He turned and jogged back down the hall to the door at the other end.

"Hey!" she called after him. "Where are you going? Will!"

He dashed through the door without looking back and ran to the parking lot. Mike sat in her car, the front door open, the photography book spread on the steering wheel, the plastic bowl of salad in her lap. She looked like an oasis.

She raised her head. "I thought you weren't coming."

"It was a narrow escape," he said, folding himself into

the passenger seat. "She asked me to her birthday party Saturday night."

"Are you going?" She kept her eyes on the book.

"I guess so. I said I would. Are you invited?"

"Be serious. But you should definitely go. See what the level of social activity is like around here. Cindy's party, at least, is different from the usual bonfire drinking parties at the dump, and jackrabbit shooting outings. You might like it."

He took a bite of his sandwich. "Are you mad at me again? What for, this time? I haven't done anything."

She slapped the book closed. "I'm afraid you *will* like it."

"Wait. I thought you could tell what I like and don't like by intuition."

"Well, I don't know how you react when your hormones are on alert."

"Who says my—I can't even say it. Don't you ever get embarrassed by some of the junk you say?"

"I'm just telling you what I think. Would you like it better if I said, 'I'm sure you'll have a lovely time with Cindy, such a fine example of young womanhood, the very one I'd pick for you myself?' "

"There must be something in between. Something involving a realistic degree of tact. You're not jealous, are you?"

"Don't be ridiculous." Color came up into her cheeks. "At least, not the way you're implying. I just hate to see you waste your time with such a bimbette."

This felt like an argument with Paige. He was being maneuvered into taking a stand defending something he didn't want to defend: Cindy.

He had an idea. "Why don't you come with me?"

"Me?" she said around a mouthful of salad. Then she laughed. "Wouldn't Cindy have a fit? I'm almost tempted."

"Then do it." He didn't like admitting he'd feel safer with her along. At least, she encouraged him to say what he thought—something he couldn't seem to do with Cindy. "We can go shopping after school for her birthday present," he said.

"We have to get her a present?"

"Sure. It's her birthday. Come on. I don't want to go there by myself, anyway."

She grinned. "Maybe your hormones aren't as alert as I thought. Okay. Let's get her something really great. Maybe some leather underwear. Maybe a whip. Maybe—"

"Mike, please. You're embarrassing me again. What about some nice handkerchiefs or a bud vase or something?"

She laughed. "Now, that certainly sounds like Cindy. Leave it to me. We'll go to Manzanita after school."

Somehow Will avoided Cindy for the rest of the day and sprinted for Mike's car the second the last bell rang. He slouched down in the seat, waiting for Mike and feeling like a criminal.

He'd never seen Mike in a better mood. She didn't put on any music. Instead, she hummed a tune of her own as they ripped along the highway to Manzanita, forty miles away and the only town anywhere in the valley with more than a grocery store.

"Oh, Cindy, Cindy," Mike sang, "happy birthday to you."

"The way you're enjoying this is making me uncomfortable. Can you be trusted to behave yourself?"

"Why, sugar," she said in a syrupy Southern accent, "don't you know me better than that?"

"That's what's got me worried."

Mike braked to a stop in Manzanita's lone shopping center, consisting of a liquor store, real-estate office, movie theater (open only on Friday and Saturday nights), café, grocery store, and a drugstore that carried everything from rental videos to lawn furniture.

Mike hopped out of the car and waited for Will. She reminded him of a racehorse prancing at the starting gate.

She wandered up and down the aisles, fingering things. "An assortment of makeup?" she mused. "Lord knows she must use it up at a great rate. How about these panties with the little ants on them? That would make a sweet gift."

"Cut it out, Mike. I hardly know her. What about this?" He held up a box of dusting powder.

"Not if you think panties are too personal. Where do you think a person puts dusting powder? *All over.*"

He dropped the box back on the shelf. "This is impossible. I don't know what to get a girl for her birthday."

"What if it was my birthday?"

Ideas jumped into his mind: photography books, blank videotapes, strange earrings, big T-shirts. "I guess I could think of something," he conceded.

"That's because you know me already," she said, sounding satisfied. "That makes buying presents easy."

He stood by a rack of books. "I don't even know what she likes to read."

"You don't even know if she *can* read," Mike said. "I rather doubt it."

"Wait," Will said. "This is pretty. What do you call this?"

"It's an atomizer. You put perfume in it and spray it on."

"I'm going to get that. It's not too personal, not too expensive, and she can give it to somebody else if she doesn't like it."

"It's not very imaginative, either, but I guess it'll do, under the circumstances. I've still got to find something, though."

"You can share this with me."

"I want my own small token. Thanks, anyway."

They each bought an ice-cream cone and carried it with them as they continued their search.

Finally Mike stopped in front of a display of stuffed animals. "A-ha," she said.

"Don't you think she's too old for a toy?"

"You're never too old for a stuffed animal. I still sleep with a teddy bear I've had all my life." She rummaged through them. "Perfect," she said, pulling out a plush pig with a big fluffy bow on top of its head.

"Oh, no, you don't," Will said. "That wouldn't be nice."

"You're right," she said, putting the pig back. "But it was very tempting." She took down a fuzzy dog with a pink ribbon around its neck. "Does this meet with your approval?" When Will nodded, she said, "I hope they have a box for it. I need to get wrapping paper, too."

She tucked the dog under her arm and marched Will to the wrapping-paper section.

All the way home, he wondered if he should have asked Mike to the party. It didn't seem that one more person would make much difference at a party, but he should probably say something about it to Cindy.

When Mike dropped him off, she said, "You want me to wrap your package? I've got lots of paper."

"Yeah, that'd be great. You sure my present's okay?"

"Stop worrying. She'll love it."

"Okay. See you tomorrow."

The next morning, they were late to school because they'd sat in the parking lot too long, finishing an argument, and Will didn't talk to Cindy until after first period.

"I missed seeing you at your locker this morning," she said. Today's color was pink.

"I was late. Say, Cindy, is it okay if I bring a friend to your party Saturday?" He knew it was cowardly of him, but he didn't want to mention Mike's name unless Cindy asked.

She thought a minute. "I guess. I can get my cousin to come, to balance things out."

"I don't want to cause you any problems. I don't have to bring—"

"No, it's okay. I want you to be happy." They went in to second period together.

13

On Saturday, Mike came by the Snakebite just at closing and helped Will clean up, even though she was dressed formally, for her, in black jeans, gray cowboy boots, and a long-sleeved gray T-shirt. Her earrings were enormous and looked like farm implements. Paige had bugged out with Timothy exactly at eight. Then Mike came back to the trailer with him while he showered and changed clothes.

Mike was sitting on his bed when he came out of the shower, a towel around his middle. "Hey, haven't you ever heard of privacy?"

"How am I ever to get educated if you don't help me? I'm from a manless household. I need to study the species in its natural habitat. Anyway, I find your chest wig fascinating."

"Huh," Will said, standing helplessly in the doorway. He was embarrassed by his hairy chest. It had happened so quickly he still wasn't used to it himself.

"Also, those biceps. They just make me feel all swoony."

"Okay, that's it," he said, holding his towel together with one hand and pulling her to her feet with the other.

"You wait outside. I can't groom myself while being observed."

"Like primitive primates," she said, as he closed the door behind her.

It was after nine-thirty when they got to Cindy's, and Will was puzzled by the quiet look of the house. He'd expected there to be other cars, lights, music.

"You sure you got the right night?" Mike asked, echoing Will's thoughts.

"I think so. Maybe everybody walked over?"

"Well, come on." She took the presents from the back seat and handed him his.

"This looks beautiful," Will said, admiring the fancy wrapping. "You did a nice job."

"Thanks."

They stood at the front door for a minute, listening, before they looked at each other, shrugged, and knocked.

Cindy opened the door. She looked first at Will and then at Mike. "I thought you said you were bringing a friend."

"I did. Mike."

"I thought you meant a guy. Not her." Cindy sounded mad. "What's my cousin going to do?"

Will was baffled. Behind Cindy, the house was dark except for the flicker of candles, and all he could hear was violin music. "Is the power out?" he asked. No, that couldn't be right. Something electric had to be playing the music.

"No, the power's not out, you dope. The candles are for atmosphere."

"Oh." He wondered if she was ever going to invite

them in. "Is everybody else here already?" Maybe the party was already over, though ten o'clock on a Saturday night was pretty early for that.

"Everybody else has been here for a long time." Her words were sarcastic.

"So, should we come in?" He felt like an idiot, standing on the doorstep, a fancy package in his hands, unable to figure out what was going on.

"Oh, all right." She opened the door enough to let them in.

It took a minute for Will's eyes to adjust to the dark. Candles burned on two or three tables and the lush music soared through the room. A girl who looked like Cindy sat on the couch, and as he looked closer, Will saw both she and Cindy wore similar dresses—tight, black, with thin straps. They both wore shiny bows in their hair. There was no one else in the room.

An idea grew in Will's head—an idea he didn't like at all. He was sure Mike had figured it out long before he did, and he had to admire her restraint. She hadn't said a single word yet. She put her present gently down on the table in front of the couch.

He cleared his throat. "Hi," he said to the girl on the couch. She lifted a hand and gave him a tiny wave. "Here," he said, thrusting the package at Cindy. "Happy birthday."

She snatched it from him.

His hands seemed big and clumsy and he stuck them in his back pockets. He couldn't imagine why Sam had ever called them careful. He thought if he took them out of his pockets, they'd flop around, breaking furniture.

Was there going to be any graceful way out of this? Cindy wasn't going to help. She just stood, holding the package and looking at him. Her cousin sat on the couch picking at a hangnail. Mike, her hands clasped in front of her, looked idly around the room. For once he wanted her to speak, and for once she wouldn't. But he knew it must be killing her to keep quiet.

"Matching wrapping paper. Isn't that cute?" Cindy said.

"I think we'd better go," he finally said. Graceful it wasn't, but he didn't think he could stand this another minute. There were a few other things he thought of to say, but they all seemed only to complicate matters more.

"I agree," Cindy said.

He and Mike let themselves out.

As soon as the door closed behind them, Will turned on Mike. "Why didn't you say something? You knew what was going on before I did."

"It was hardly my place to say anything," she snapped. "That whole deal was between you and Cindy. I was an innocent bystander. I have to confess, though, I was awfully tempted."

"God, I can't believe she'd do something like that in front of other people. It was so . . . so—"

"Tawdry?" Mike offered. "Tacky? Flagrant? Vulgar? Sleazy?"

"One of those."

"Probably all of them," Mike said, getting into the car. "Oh, what a trap she had set for you. Just like a spider, sitting in the middle of that candlelit web. I have to say, it was very thoughtful of her to provide a companion for your friend. If only she'd had Spike Winslow there instead of her cousin, we could have stayed."

"Who's Spike Winslow?"

"Tackle on the football team. Pure USDA choice, but he's gorgeous."

"I don't care who else she had there. No way was I staying. I didn't know you lusted for this Spike." He couldn't understand why he felt put out at the idea of Mike and this Winslow person.

"Purely animal attraction. He's incapable of coherent conversation, but there are certain circumstances, I'm led to believe, in which coherent conversation is irrelevant. And I think what Cindy had set up there for you was one of those circumstances. I certainly hope I didn't spoil things for you by going along. I can drop you back there if you like."

He groaned.

"Is that a no? Poor Cindy. I think her vanity's going to be rather bruised."

"If you don't shut up, you're going to get bruised."

"Tell me, big boy, have you ever been in love?"

"I'm warning you."

"I'm serious. Have you?"

"Have you?"

"I asked you first."

"Don't you have any restraint?"

"How can you ask that? You'll never see me any more restrained than I was in that lovely candlelit room."

"No," he almost shouted. "I've never been in love. I suppose that makes me socially retarded."

"Then that's two of us," she said quietly. "It's not a crime."

He thought for a minute. "Let's go back to the Snakebite. I'll open up the milk-shake machine for us."

"Deal."

They were sitting at the counter over chocolate milk shakes when Timothy and Paige came in the back door.

"I saw the lights on in here," Paige said. "What's going on?"

"Midnight snack," Will told her. "Want some?"

"On the house?" Timothy asked. When Will nodded, he sat on a counter stool. "In that case. Sit down, pretty Paige."

Will made the milk shakes, set them before Paige and Timothy, and sat down again. "The four basic food groups," he said. "Sugar, salt, grease, and caffeine. Drink up."

"And what have you merry children been up to tonight?" Timothy asked.

"We went to a party," Will said.

"It wasn't very exciting, though," Mike said.

"And drinking milk shakes is?" Paige asked.

Will and Mike caught each other's eyes and laughed.

Monday morning, Will was relieved to find no Cindy at his locker. He knew he'd have to see her in first period, but he wouldn't have to talk to her.

He was already in his seat when she came through the classroom door. She saw him, wound up, and lobbed Mike's stuffed dog across the room at him. She waited long enough to see it bounce off his head, then swiveled and left the classroom.

Curious faces turned in Will's direction from all over the room. He picked up the dog, shrugged in an embarrassed way, and sat down, wishing he could disappear. The teacher's entrance diverted attention from him, but all through the class, heads periodically turned to look at him and the fuzzy animal on his desk.

As soon as he entered second period, he strode to Mike's desk and plopped the dog down on her big black bag.

"Where'd you get that?" Mike asked.

"Cindy showed up in first period just long enough to throw it at me." He looked around for her, wondering if she would attack again, but didn't see her.

"I guess she didn't like it, then. Too bad. Maybe she thought it was a female dog and misunderstood."

"A female dog? Oh, you mean a b—" Will said. "Mike! You didn't mean for her to think that, did you?"

"Of course not," she said, looking Will directly in the eye. "I just thought it would be a cute present. I have no control over my subconscious, though. Did she keep the atomizer?"

"Thank goodness. She could have really hurt me with that. What I'd like to know is why she didn't throw it at you."

"A woman scorned takes it out on the scorner. I'm just glad I didn't give her a bowling ball."

"*You're* glad. Well, I guess that's the end of my social life around here."

"Oh, don't worry about it. I'll be your friend, no matter what unsavory types you choose to scorn. You're not going to be in Sand Land long enough to care, anyhow. You'll be out of here come June, and between the Snakebite and Sam's house and me, you'll have plenty to keep you busy until then."

The final bell rang, without Cindy's arrival. She must have decided to cut the whole day. Will dropped into his seat, aware that Mike's promise of friendship soothed the wound to his ego Cindy had inflicted.

14

In two evenings Sam was able to teach Will the simple cuts with gouge and chisel that, when repeated with variations, would make the decorative designs for the lintels and vigas.

Will felt a swelling pride when Sam stood over him, nodding approval as he made the hard straight downward cuts across the grain of the pine practice board, and then the easy shallow sloping cuts with the grain, lifting and removing the waste wood. He loved the feel of the tools in his hand, the smell of cut wood, the way the design grew from his own effort. He loved, too, the way Sam would rest his hand on Will's shoulder as he watched him work, the way he kept saying, "You're a natural, boy," the satisfaction Sam seemed to get from Will's progress.

Whenever Will stopped to rest his hands, he and Sam sketched possible designs of carvings for the house.

"Now, an adobe house, properly done, is somewhere between shelter and art," Sam told him, "and you won't find any sharp edges. Not in mine, anyway. There's no sharp edges in this desert landscape, you see. It flows and rolls, sort of like a well-built woman, if you take my meaning." He winked at Will. "I always like a curved line better than a straight one myself. What about you?"

"I never thought about it," Will said. "But I guess that's one of the things I like about the ocean—the curves and rolls."

"And about your friend Cindy?"

"Well, Cindy, she and I aren't, well—" and he told Sam about the birthday party.

Sam threw his head back and laughed. "I guess that solves your problem of putting some distance between you and Cindy. And what did you think about all that?"

"I felt like the village idiot. I think Mike knew what was up as soon as we got there, and I was still trying to figure it out when we left. I can't believe I asked Cindy if there'd been a power failure when I saw all those candles. God!"

"So you're on Miss Cindy's blacklist."

"That's okay with me." He didn't want to say Cindy's boldness scared him, or that he was glad Mike had been with him that night. It made him sound like a wimp. "She's on mine. I didn't like the way she bounced that dog off my skull."

"It salved her pride, boy. Now you've embarrassed each other and you're even." He laughed again. "I sure would like to have seen your face once you got the lay of the land."

"I'm glad you couldn't. I doubt it was a pretty sight."

They turned back to their work. "As I was saying," Sam said, "I like a curved line better than a straight one, and so I want these designs to be curvy."

By the end of the second evening, they'd decided on

the designs and Sam packed the tools Will would need to take to the house.

"Tomorrow, out at the site, I'll label which are the window lintels and which are for the doors. We'll need to put those up first before the vigas, so you'll have to get going."

"I'll come straight after school every day, I promise," Will said. He could hardly wait to get started making the corner rosettes and twisted channeling they'd finally decided on.

Will was as good as his word. He and Mike went to the adobe site directly after school, his tools and her camera on the floor in the back seat of the VW. Sam stopped work when they arrived, to have a quick snack with them from his cooler, and then they went to work.

The warm dry weather held, but the November sunsets came early and there was no time to waste not working. Mike, when she wasn't filming, helped Sam lay plumbing lines and electrical wires while Will carved. The more he did, the faster he got, and they toasted themselves with apple cider when they set the first lintel over the front door. Will thought it was the most beautiful doorframe he'd ever seen.

At night he was often at Sam's, working on a collection of carved desert animals. His skill improved rapidly from the daily practice, and he could work for over an hour before he needed a break. As he rested and flexed his hands, he admired the assortment of kangaroo rats, roadrunners, snakes, coyotes, and jackrabbits he'd created. His current project was a pair of what Mike called l.g.b.s—the little gray birds that nested in the dune primrose.

On weekends, Will cooked and sweated all day and chafed at not being able to be at the site with Mike and Sam. He'd finished the lintels and begun on the vigas, which were the width of a room and would take a long time to do.

While he cooked, he would try to imagine what Mike and Sam were doing, based on what he knew of their plans for the day. He got so good at it that at times he was almost positive he could see Sam, hear him grunt as he lifted a brick, see him dust his hands and smile with satisfaction when the brick was set, watch the patch of sweat on the back of his shirt grow. And always, Mike behind the camera, squinting and filming.

Mr. Hintz, the Snakebite's owner, had returned from his trip and had spent a lot of time at the café, watching Will and Paige work. Will didn't do much differently than he usually did, but Paige was abnormally cheerful and efficient. After about two weeks, Mr. Hintz had told them they were wonderful, and to call him if they encountered any problems; he was going to be spending most of his time restoring old cars. After that, they saw him only at the end of the month, when he came in to do the Snakebite's books.

One November Monday there was a school holiday for some kind of teachers' meeting, and since the Snakebite was always closed on Monday, Will had the whole day to work on the adobe. He woke up feeling like it was Christmas morning.

Mike picked him up at the usual time and they even beat Sam to the house.

As Mike wandered into the roofless structure and disappeared, Will stood alone and looked. It was the first time he'd seen the house in early light. In the still, golden desert morning, the mud-brick house did seem to be growing out of the earth, pushing its way from beneath the sand, finding its place in the harmony of the landscape.

He was not unaware of the beauty and power of the desert, especially at night, but for the first time he had a sense of its pull on a person's heart, the same way the sea pulled him. He suddenly understood, from what Mike had taught him about film, that the desert was the negative image of the sea. Silent and gilded opposed to sibilant and blue-green-gray; dry opposite wet; stillness against motion; both shining, vast, ancient and elemental, both mysterious with secret life; poles of the same living, breathing world. He felt a kinship with Sam in the landscapes of their souls. Even if Paige learned nothing from coming to this place, he knew he had.

"Are you going to stand there all day looking like you've been hit over the head?" Mike asked, coming out of the adobe. "What's wrong?"

"Nothing. I was just admiring this beautiful house." However much Mike might believe in the importance of sharing every thought in her head, he knew there would always be some of his own that he kept to himself. Because he didn't know how to put them into words, or because he was afraid he'd be misunderstood, or for some other reason, he wasn't sure. But he knew he wasn't going to talk about his new feelings of respect for the desert with someone who called it Sand Land.

They turned at the sound of Sam's truck arriving, and their workday began.

By midafternoon, Will's shoulders and arms ached and sweat dripped into his eyes in spite of the bandana he had tied around his forehead. He couldn't remember why he'd thought the desert had any kind of allure at all, and he was tired of Mike's constant energetic chatter. He preferred Sam's deliberateness, his ability to communicate what needed to be done with a gesture or a single syllable. He thought he could work by Sam's side into eternity without losing his temper, and after less than one full day of Mike, he was ready to bind and gag her.

She buzzed around them like a mayfly trying to pack a lifetime of living into its one day of life. It seemed that every time Will or Sam turned around, they were looking into the lens of her camera.

"Pain," she'd say. "I want to see pain on those faces. What kind of documentary will this be if you make it look easy? This is the kind of a project only a special hardy few take on. Make it look easy and everybody and his cousin Jack will be trying it. And you don't want that, do you? This desert'll be full of bozos throwing up adobe condominiums and adobe hot tubs and adobe health spas. Doesn't that make you . . ."

"Don't you ever get tired?" Will burst out. "I never knew anybody who could talk the way you do."

"*I* don't see how the two of you can work for hours without saying *anything*. Don't you want to communicate with each other? How do you know you're still *there*?"

"Come on, Will," Sam said. "Let's take a break while I tell Mike the facts of life." He dragged a bandana from his pocket and mopped his face while he pulled a root beer from the cooler. He sat down in the shade of the house and said, "Come over here, honey, and let me tell you about the difference between boys and girls."

"I know the difference," Mike said, continuing to film Sam as he sat down. She zoomed in on his face as he took a swig from his root beer. "In theory, anyway."

"Turn that thing off. I'm starting to feel like you've got my whole life on film. I look over my shoulder for you when I step in the shower. Now sit down here, honey, and let's do some communicating."

Mike sat down next to him. "Okay. Shoot." She wiggled her shoulders contentedly. "I love this kind of a talk."

"I know you do. And that's the difference I want to tell you about. Men, in general, *don't* love this kind of a talk."

"But why not?" She sat up straighter. "How do men get to know each other?"

"They hang out together. Play basketball together. Drink a beer together."

"Whittle together?" she asked pointedly. "Build a house together?"

"A couple of very good ways," he agreed. "You can learn a lot about somebody by watching the way he works. Our friend Will here has careful hands. I knew that the first time I saw him cook."

"But that's so . . . so oblique. Isn't it simpler to say, 'Tell me, how do you feel about whatever'?"

"Well, men do that sometimes, too, honey. They just aren't as comfortable plowing around in each other's heads, the way a lot of women like to do. And they especially don't want to plow around in their own feelings, much less someone else's."

"But it's better that way," Mike insisted. "I like to hear about everything that's going on with somebody else—what they think about when they're not really thinking about anything, what's their favorite breakfast, what's the worst thing their parents ever did to them. When I'm being friends with somebody, I want to turn them inside out and know everything."

"Where'd you learn that?" Sam asked. "Is that how your mom is?"

"No," Mike said, more slowly. "She's more like you say a man is. But she's that way with everything else, too. She's missing the stuff I like, the closeness, the involvement, the connecting."

"So where'd you learn it? Who did that with you?"

"Nobody. I just did it naturally. That's me."

"That's why I think it's a natural difference," Sam said. "For most people. Marcella may be an exception, like she is in just about everything else."

Paige, too, Will thought.

"It probably goes back a long, long time," Sam went on, "to when men were sneaking around behind trees looking for a saber-tooth tiger, being quiet and keeping a close eye on the guy guarding their back, and women were back at the campfire singing to babies and keeping each other company."

"That's about the most sexist thing I ever heard," Mike said. "Not to mention the way you keep calling me honey. You don't call Will honey."

"You're right. I call him boy. You want me to start

calling you that? You want me to stop calling you honey?"

"No. I like you to call me honey. But I know it's *me* you're calling that, and not every woman you see."

"That's right, honey. Well, you may think that caveman stuff is sexist, but I think that's how it was, and is, and I think it's because men and women are different and that's all there is to it."

"Well, I think that's a cop-out manufactured by men who don't want to be bothered changing. What's a woman supposed to do when she's got a man she wants to communicate with and he won't?"

"Make it easy for him. Don't scare him with it. Pretend you're trying to tame a skittish tomcat."

"That sounds sexist, too. Why shouldn't he come halfway?"

"Because he won't. And if you're going to get some of what you want out of him, you'll have to lure him sweetly into it."

"Oh, bull pucky. Sexist again. And old-fashioned."

"Well, I'm an old-fashioned guy. Now, I'm all for equal pay and equal rights under the law and all that, but I don't want us to forget that part of the fun of being men and being women is we're different."

"Were you ever married, Sam?"

"That's the kind of question another man would never ask me. He'd wait for me to volunteer it, and if I never did, he'd figure he didn't need to know it."

"You've just finished telling me how different men and women are from each other, so you can't shame me into withdrawing the question. Were you?"

Sam laughed. "Yes, I was. But you've already guessed that, haven't you?"

Mike nodded. "Didn't she teach you anything about really communicating?"

"She tried. I wasn't very cooperative."

"I bet."

"And finally we came to something we couldn't communicate about at all."

"What?"

"Now, that's something I don't want to talk about." He put his empty can down on the sand. "Nothing personal about you, honey. I just don't want to talk about it."

"I respect that. You know I'm dying to know and I'll spend the rest of my days trying to pry—excuse me. I mean lure it sweetly out of you." She gave him a sappy smile and fluttered her eyelashes.

"You got any thoughts on the matter, Will?" Sam asked. "Anything I might have missed?"

"Nope."

"You mean, I said it all just the way you would have?"

"Yep."

"See there, honey? A man can understand another man with few words. How come you females take so all-fired many?"

"There's not a one-word answer. It's just better."

Sam stood up and dusted off his jeans. "Okay, then. We men have got work to do."

Feeling satisfied and manly, Will ambled over to the wheelbarrow he'd left standing beside the viga pile.

15

As the sun flattened out on the mountain rim and bathed them and the house in ruddy light, they put away their tools and headed for home.

"I'll be over later," Will told Sam as he got into the orange VW.

When they approached the Snakebite, Mike floored the accelerator and they zoomed past it, on down the road.

"Hey," Will said. "I thought you were taking me home."

"I'm not ready yet," she said. "I'm not through talking."

He groaned.

She stopped the car at the side of the road. "I want to take a walk. I have something to tell you."

"A walk? It's almost dark. Can't we talk inside the car?"

She opened her door. "Get out. Exercise that doesn't benefit your biceps won't kill you."

"You are the bossiest female alive," he said, getting out of the car.

They walked straight into the desert from the highway. Little rustles—lizards? l.g.b.s? venomous diamondback rattlers?—came from the creosote and mesquite bushes around them, but Mike kept marching along, her jeans brushing the branches.

Will jogged to catch up with her. He knew he wouldn't have to ask her what was on her mind. Although he agreed with Sam about the differences in the way men and women related, he still liked her forthrightness. She was right—men did communicate obliquely with each other, and he wasn't always sure he made the correct interpretation. With her, there was never any doubt. She made it easy.

The sun was behind the mountains now, and their violet shadows spread across the pungent desert, while their edges were still rimmed in gold. Moment by moment, the shadows thickened and the gold lost its luster.

"Yeah?" he said.

"I put my application to UCLA in the mail this morning. I sent the house video with it, as much as I have of it. I left the ending kind of open—like a cliff-hanger. Will the house get finished or not? I told them if they accepted me I'd let them see the end."

"You think that'll help?"

"How do I know? It's worth a try. This movie looks like a thriller, not just pictures of people piling up bricks and wood. I put in shots at sunrise and sunset, and trick shots—I speeded up all that footage of you building the back wall, so you look like a brick-laying Tasmanian devil. I even went back at night and took shots with a red filter of the desert animals exploring through the house. One night a coyote sat right in the living room and howled up at the moon through the open roof. It was great. They'll have to let me in."

"Did you apply anywhere else?"

"Why? I want to go to UCLA. There's other film schools, but I want to go to UCLA."

"But what if you don't get in there?"

"Then I'll make another movie, and I'll make it even better than the house movie, which is already damn good, and I'll apply again for the next semester. And I'll keep doing that until they give up and let me in. That's what I want."

He kicked a rock ahead of him as they walked along.

"Haven't you mailed your application yet?" she asked.

"What's the point? There's no money, and what would I do about Paige?"

"But you've gone to all the trouble of filling it out, and the financial-aid forms, too, and getting your transcripts and everything. If you have to have Paige around underfoot all the time, let her go where you want to for a change."

"You don't know what you're talking about."

"Just mail it. If you get accepted, if UCLA would have the dubious taste to take you, *then* you could figure out how to do it. Come *on*, what's the problem?"

"Why set myself up to be disappointed? I've had enough of that already. Being realistic is just as important as taking chances."

"But you could . . ."

"Look, Mike, give it a rest, okay? I know what I'm doing."

"Okay, okay. But would you just tell me one thing?"

He shook his head resignedly. "You never quit, do you?"

"If you *did* get to college, let's just be hypothetical here, if you did get in, what do you think it would be like?"

"How do I know? I haven't thought about it."

"Well, think about it. How do you imagine it?"

He sighed. "Okay. Let's see. Big buildings. Lots of people. Classrooms. What else? Books. Lots of books. And a lot of large guys with muscles between their ears wearing football suits, yelling obnoxious comments to blond girls walking to class."

"Am I going to have to hurt you to get a straight answer?" She gave him a poke in the ribs.

"I don't know what to say."

"Stop whining. I'll give you some ideas. A place where you can learn about yourself. A place where you can meet people who can help you do that. A place where you can figure out how you want to be in the world, and learn what you need to do it, and learn about things you never heard of before. And where I can learn to make exciting films."

"You can do all that without college."

"Maybe. Maybe not. But not as well, not as efficiently, not as easily."

"I have the feeling you're lecturing me."

"I *am* lecturing you, you lunkhead. If you can't tell when you're being lectured, I guess you're better off not going to college."

He stopped and turned to face her in the fading light. Quietly he said, "I'd love to go to college. I'd love to do all the things you said, as well as all the fun stuff—parties and football games and stupid pranks. I don't have any idea what I'd major in, but I'd love to take a lot of different classes, to learn about everything. But I can't. Not now, and maybe not ever. I have other things I have to take care of first. So you can lecture me until you run out of wind and it won't change the fact that I can't go to college now. So would you please stop talking about it? It's hard for me to listen."

She put her hand on his arm. "Oh, Will. I'm sorry." Then she hit herself in the forehead with her palm. "I can be such a dope. Such an insensitive, obtuse, heartless, unsympathetic, cruel, unfeeling dope."

"Come on, Mike. It's not that bad."

"I feel like a creep. I just wanted to share this whole college thing with you. I wanted you to go to UCLA with me. I didn't mean to hurt you."

"Stop groveling, will you, before I, in my inarticulate, bewildered male way, express myself with violence, the last resort of a dumb, harassed animal."

"Oh, shut up. Anyway, if you try violence with me, you'll find your nose in the sand."

"Yeah, right."

"Listen, you. My whole body is a lethal weapon. I took a self-defense class last year and now *nobody* messes with me."

"And how many people messed with you before?"

"Well, none, actually."

"So, you don't know if it works or not, do you?"

"Why are you looking at me like that? I know it works." She took a couple of steps away from him. "You don't want to get hurt, do you? Hey!"

He grabbed her from behind, pinning her arms to her sides and pressing her into the ground so she couldn't lift her feet to kick. She jerked her head backward, but it only thudded awkwardly against his chest.

"Let me go! Stop it! I'm not kidding!"

He released her. "I believe I've made my point."

"Oh, don't you look so smug. That was an awful thing to do." Mike's eyes glistened with tears in the dimness. "The fact that you can overpower me physically doesn't mean anything."

Baffled, Will spread his hands out at his sides. "I thought we were kidding around. Did I hurt you?"

"You could have if you wanted to. Isn't that what you were trying to prove? Do you have any idea how sick I am of being dismissed and disregarded because I'm five feet tall and weigh a hundred pounds? Bulk and brute strength aren't everything, you know." The tears slid down her cheeks and dropped off her chin into the sand.

"Hey, Mike." He reached his hand out to her, but she slapped it away. "I'm sick to death of being treated like some stupid child, to be humored and then dismissed. I'm going to put my images up on a screen so they're thirty feet high. Then maybe somebody'll take me seriously."

Will took her shoulders and pulled her gradually closer to him until her forehead was against his shirt, and he could feel her tears soaking through it to his skin. "This isn't all because I grabbed you. What's going on, Mike?"

She pushed her hands between his shirt and her face and cried into her palms. "It's that dumb dig of hers," she sobbed. "I haven't been filming it, the way she wants me to, so she's taking away the camera. Today was my last chance, and I used it filming the house instead of for her. She won't give it back to me until I promise to finish filming the dig in time for this presentation she has to give in April."

"But I thought you'd agreed to film the dig as a condition of getting the camera."

"That's true," she sniffled. "But I don't want to. It's so boring. And it's for *her*."

"But you said you'd do it. You have to."

"Whose side are you on, anyway?" She drew away from him.

"It's not a matter of sides. Your mother bought you that camera—and those babies aren't cheap—to do a job for her, not to run all over, shooting for fun. You have to do the job." He paused. "How about if I help you?"

She looked up at him, her face streaked with tear tracks. "You? How can you help me?"

"I'll keep you company. I'll brainstorm with you. I'll draw title boards. I'll . . . I don't know. Whatever you need."

"You will?" She scrubbed her cheeks with the heels of her hands.

"Why not? We're . . . you know. That F word. Aren't we?"

She nodded, her forehead bumping his chest.

"But don't worry," she said, sounding like her tough, dauntless self again. "I'll keep your nasty little secret. We wouldn't want it to get out that you were my . . . you know. That F word."

16

By the middle of December, the exterior walls were complete, the doors and windows in place, the bond beam poured, and the ceiling plate in place. The roof was to be a traditional Pueblo-style flat roof, with the round vigas forming the ceiling and roof foundation.

Will had almost finished the carving on the vigas and, with Sam's help, hoped to have them done by Christmas vacation, when they planned to begin roofing. The main problem on Sam's mind was how to raise the vigas to the roof without calling in outside help. He was obsessive about only the three of them, he, Will, and Mike, touching his house.

Mike spent a couple of afternoons trailing after her mother at Marcella's Indian site, halfheartedly taking pictures, but it was enough to get her the camera back.

After her second excursion with Marcella, she came to Sam's to join him and Will for dinner, the camera cradled in her arms.

"Look what I've got," she crowed, and kissed the top of the camera. "You're not safe in the shower anymore."

"How did it go?" Sam asked, coming out of the kitchen, an apron around his waist.

"B-o-o-o-o-ring," she said. "I simply cannot get

worked up about a couple of bedrock mortars and some ancient pottery chips. It's so typical of her to only be interested in things that can't talk back. What's for dinner?"

"Spaghetti," Sam said.

"Don't let him kid you," Will said. "It's spaghetti noodles, all right, but the sauce is that lethal chili of his. I brought a fire extinguisher."

"What have you guys been doing while I've been five million years away?"

"Carving vigas and trying to figure out how to get them up," Sam said. "Once you two are out for Christmas vacation, I ought to have a plan."

"Unfortunately, I'll have to miss the serious bodily harm I'm sure it will entail. Marcella's dragging me off to have Christmas with the relatives," Mike said. "I just hope this good weather holds for you. Last year at this time, it was too windy to step outside unless you wanted your skin sanded off."

Will wandered into the workshop as Mike and Sam talked in the kitchen. He liked to be amid the wood smells and the tidy rows of tools. The finished and in-progress carvings lining the workbench pleased his eye and gave him a feeling of continuity. He rearranged his ranks of carved animals.

"Hey, Sam," he said, going back into the living room. "What happened to my kangaroo rat? The one holding the piñon nut?"

"I don't know. It's got to be in there somewhere."

"And didn't I have another rattlesnake, a big one?"

"I can't keep up with you, you're making them so fast.

We'll dig around after dinner. I'm sure we'll find them. Come sit down now. Dinner's ready."

After dinner, Mike and Will worked out designs for the title boards he was making for Marcella's video, and when they finished that, Mike took him home.

The wind came up during the first day of Christmas vacation, dropping the temperature and driving such amounts of scouring sand that work on the house was impossible. Sam and Will battened down the tarps covering their equipment and went home, hoping for better weather the next day.

They didn't get it. For two weeks, the weather stayed the same—howling wind and hard blue sky. Sam paced restlessly around the trailer, stroking his mustache and muttering, unable to concentrate enough to whittle. Will kept him company sometimes, but the howling of the wind made him jittery too, and they decided they were better off apart, since they only compounded each other's overstrung nervousness. Sam's lectures about the various winds of the world—the Mexican chubasco, the Mediterranean sirocco and mistral, the Italian tramontana, the African simoom—only increased their awareness of the screaming blasts.

Will spent the time taking long naps and catching up on the homework he'd let slide in spending so much time at the adobe. Christmas passed almost unnoticed.

The day school started again in January, the wind stopped, the sun shone, and the air was mild. Perfect roofing weather.

After school, Will and Mike went straight to the house

site, to find Sam sitting on one of the boulders he'd been collecting to landscape the finished house.

"I've got a plan," he told them as they got out of the car.

"For the vigas?" Will asked.

"No, not yet. Anyway, I don't want to start that if there's a chance of the wind coming up again. It'd blow them right off the roof and into next week. We need a good stretch of quiet weather for that. What I thought we'd do is arrange some of these boulders. Kind of get an idea of how they'll look, scattered artfully around." At Will's skeptical expression, he said, "Think of your biceps, boy. This'll put the final polish on them."

"I'll take lots of nice pictures," Mike said. "You just go right ahead and flex those itty-bitty biceps of yours, and I'll get the whole pitiful thing on film."

"Hold on," Will said. "You must be mistaking my massive arms for those belonging to some pantywaist among your acquaintance."

Mike coughed behind her hand. "Dear me. Have I hit a nerve?" She squeezed his arm. "Maybe I was wrong. There might be something in there after all. Somewhere."

"Look who's talking. You and those toothpick arms. I don't understand how you're even able to lift that camera."

"You ever hear of tensile strength? Here, take a feel." She pulled her shirtsleeve back and held her arm out to him.

Will turned to Sam. "This happens to me all the time. Women come up to me on the street and say that to me. Here, take a feel. It's a curse." He touched Mike's arm with his thumb and forefinger as if he were pinching a twig. "Ooooh."

"Children," Sam said. "It'll be dark before the two of you quit arguing over whose muscles are bigger. Or smaller. Anyway, I'll need both of you to push those things around."

"Me?" Mike squeaked. "You want me to do brainless labor? Dirty my hands? Please. I'm an artist."

"Get over here, Ms. Artist, honey, and lean some of that tensile strength against one of these rocks. I want the first one over there by the road."

"That's nothing for a stud like me," Will said, pressing his palms against the rock and pushing. The rock didn't move. He turned his back to it and pushed from that angle, and still it didn't move.

Mike came to stand beside him. She spit on her palms, rubbed them together, placed them on the rock, and said, "Okay. Now!"

Together the three of them pushed, and slowly the rock moved across the sand.

"It's me, of course." Mike panted, pushing.

"Save your breath," Sam gasped.

As they got the boulder to its resting place, Will said, "We did that so well, I think we ought to form a rock group."

Mike and Sam began laughing in great gusts as they slid down, their backs against the rock, and sat on the sand, still laughing.

"Great idea," Mike said. "You can be W-I-L and I'll be M-Y-K and Sam can be . . . Sam can be Fifi. Weird names are important in the music business."

"Fifi? Do I look like a Fifi to you?"

"It doesn't mean anything. The Thompson Twins were a trio, and one of them was black. The gimmick's what's important."

"Okay. I'll be Fifi. We'll be Fifi and His Kids. We can bring our own rocks." Sam got up, dug a piece of yellow surveyor's chalk from his pocket, and went to write on a viga. He stepped back to admire the big yellow letters between Will's carved designs: FIFI AND HIS KIDS, WIL AND MYK.

Mike ran to get her camera and slowly panned the viga, murmuring into the microphone, "This was the beginning. Who could know that, from such a humble start, international stars would be born."

"Come on," Sam said. "Let's move a few more before it gets dark. Stardom awaits."

The next day, when Mike and Will arrived at the construction site, Sam's truck wasn't there. The day was gray and cool, but without wind.

"You think he decided it's too cold to work?" Mike asked.

Will shrugged. "Why don't we go by the trailer and see if he's there."

Mike turned the car around and they drove back to the main highway and to Sam's. The truck was parked outside. He hollered to them to come on in when Mike knocked. They found him sitting in his chair whittling over a newspaper spread in his lap, his left foot in a cast propped on a footstool.

"Sam! What happened?"

"A stupid accident. I was too impatient to get one of those vigas up. I just didn't want to wait any longer. So

I laid it across the top of one of those 55-gallon drums, thinking I could raise one end by pushing down on the other, and when it was higher than the top of the wall, I'd pivot it on the drum and swing it over and down onto the top of the wall. Then I could heave the lower end up until the whole thing fell across the angle of the corner and then climb up and roll it to where I wanted it. Moving those rocks must have gone to my head. Anyway, I got it up and leaning on the wall before my arms gave out, and when it fell, I didn't get out of the way fast enough and it fell on my foot. I'll be in this thing for six weeks."

"Oh, no," Mike wailed. "Now you'll have to hire somebody to do it."

"No way. It can just wait until I'm better. Nobody else is touching my house. This'll give me time to figure out how to do it."

"But six weeks," Mike said.

"Not much in geologic time," Sam told her. "Ask your mother."

Mike made a face.

"I wasn't able to cover everything before I dragged myself into the truck and off to the doctor. I was kind of hoping you two might be able to go out to the house and take care of that for me."

"You should have waited for my biceps, Sam," Will said.

Mike snickered, ignored the look Will gave her, and said, "Sure, we'll take care of it. We can do it now, before it gets dark. It won't take long. Then we'll come back and see you."

"I'll stop at the Snakebite and pick up some burgers

for dinner," Will said. "I don't guarantee they'll taste the same cooked in your antiseptic kitchen as they do in the rancid grease of the Snakebite's grill, but you can't have everything. And I'd just as soon avoid that chili of yours for a while."

17

The first few days, Will and Mike went straight to Sam's after school to keep him company, run errands, and fix his dinner.

But Sam seemed distant and preoccupied, unwilling to talk much, preferring to lie watching TV, his cast up on the couch arm.

Even Mike, with her considerable communicative abilities, couldn't reach him.

"Hey, Sam, are you in there?" she'd ask, and he'd grunt in response.

"Does your foot hurt? You want a pain pill?"

"No."

"You need anything from the store?"

"No."

"Sam, this is Mike here. Talk to me."

"Got nothing to say. I'm resting."

As they got ready to leave on Thursday of the first week, Will reminded Sam, "You know I can't come by tomorrow. I have to help Paige at the Snakebite."

"Okay. You don't need to come either, Mike. I'm fine."

"Well, all right," she said hesitantly. "I'll wait until Saturday morning to check on you."

"No need for that. I'll call you if I need anything."

"You mean you don't want us to come by at all?" She sounded shocked.

"I can't see any reason you need to." He kept his eyes on the TV.

"How about because I want to?"

"I'll call you if I need anything," he repeated.

Mike opened her mouth to try again, but Will touched her arm and shook his head at her. She looked at him, her face full of questions, and he jerked his head toward the door.

"Bye, Sam," he said. "We'll be seeing you."

When they were outside, Mike hissed at him, "What's going on? What's wrong with him?"

"I don't know," Will said, getting in the car. "But whatever it is, isn't it obvious he doesn't want to tell us?"

"What's that got to do with anything? He has to tell us. That's what friends are for."

"Remember what he said that day at the site—that if there's something he won't tell you, then it's something you don't need to know."

"I don't want you taking this strong silent business of his too seriously," Mike said. "You can see how far it's gotten him. He's living all alone in a hostile environment."

"His choice, Mike. People get to choose their own lives."

"Is that what you want for yours? If not, you better improve those communication skills. I don't like this withdrawal of his. It's not healthy. I bet you could get it out of him, man to man."

"But I won't. He's brooding about something and

that's his business. Just because you're so darned curious about everybody's inner workings doesn't mean they've got to tell you."

"I'd tell, if it was me." She pressed harder on the accelerator and Will winced. Why did she always drive as fast as she talked?

"Well, not everybody's like you."

"You were about to add, 'Thank goodness,' weren't you?"

"No." He had been.

"Huh. If you find out anything, I want you to tell me right away. I'm worried about him."

Will knew she was. So was he. But he also knew that if Sam told him anything, he'd keep it to himself. Anything Sam wanted Mike to know, *he'd* have to tell her.

Friday night after the Snakebite closed, Will paced around the empty trailer for an hour before he decided he wasn't going to be able to relax enough to sleep. Maybe a walk in the desert would help.

The night was cold but piercingly clear, aromatic with desert plants, and as silent as ever. Before he realized it, he was on his way to Sam's. When he reached the trailer, he stood outside, just looking. It was late, but the lights were on inside. He knew he shouldn't, but he couldn't seem to help himself: he stepped up to the door and rapped softly.

He thought he heard a sound from inside, the sound of something falling to the floor. He knocked again, louder, and this time was answered by a groan. He tried the door. It wasn't locked, so he pushed it open slowly.

Sam lay on his stomach on the couch, one hand hanging to the floor next to an overturned bottle. Three beer bottles stood on the table in front of the couch.

"Sam? Are you okay?"

The room had a heavy, stale smell, and it was very warm. Sam's foot, in its cast, was hooked over the arm of the couch.

He raised his head and squinted at Will. "Kevin?" he asked, his voice slurred. He tried to turn over, to sit up, but the cast prevented him. "Oh, God, Kevin." His voice broke on a sob. "I'm sorry."

"It's Will, Sam." He stood by the couch, his hands at his sides. He felt big and hot and clumsy and he didn't know what to do.

"Will?" He gave up struggling to sit up and lay quietly, his eyes moist and unfocused.

"Yeah. I was just taking a walk and didn't realize I was heading in this direction until I was already here. I know you said not to come by, and I didn't really mean to. I mean, it was almost an accident I'm here"—he knew he was babbling but he couldn't stop—"and then I heard a funny noise and I was afraid something was wrong, so I—"

"Help me sit up, Will." His voice was low and slurred.

Will moved Sam's legs and then took him under the arms, levering him into a sitting position. "Can I . . . is there anything I can get you?"

"Glass of water, please." Sam put his elbows on his knees and held his head in his hands.

Will came from the kitchenette with a tall glass of water. He held it out to Sam, who didn't raise his head, so Will put the glass down on the coffee table and stood with his hands in his back pockets. "I guess I'd better go now."

"No." Sam cleared his throat. "Sit down."

Will dropped into the chair across from the sofa. He wasn't sure his watery knees would have gotten him as far as the front door anyhow. Neither of them spoke for several minutes.

Then Sam lifted his head and shook it slowly. "I thought you were Kevin."

Will cleared his throat. "Who's Kevin?"

"Kevin is my son. He was killed in Vietnam on this day. Before you were even born." He took the glass of water in a shaky hand and drank it all.

"I'm sorry."

"I'm sorry, too." He rolled the glass between his palms. "But he wanted to go. She wanted him to go to college in Canada, where he'd be safe, but he didn't want that. He knew he wasn't cut out for college, and the life ahead of him looked pretty ordinary. He wanted his chance at some kind of glory. I understood that, so we both fought her on it. And we won, if you can call it that." The glass fell from his hands, hit the bottle, and broke between Sam's feet, but he didn't seem to notice. "She never forgave me. And I can't forgive myself."

"You did what you thought was best." Was that the right thing to say? Will didn't know.

"But I was wrong. If I'd insisted, he would have gone to Canada. He listened to me."

"He might not have, that time," Will said hesitantly. Mike would know what to say, but he didn't. "You said he wanted to go."

Sam shook his head. "He'd still be alive. That was the most important thing."

Will looked at his hands in his lap. For months after his mother died, he'd ransacked his mind for ways he might have saved her. Another doctor, a different treatment, a better hospital, even though it was already too late.

"He's safe now," Will said, the same thing he'd finally had to say about his mother.

Sam lowered his face into his hands again, and his shoulders shook.

"You need to get some sleep." Will stood up and helped Sam to his feet. "Come on." He led him to the bedroom and sat him on the bed. Doing something physical was always easier than talking about difficult things, especially when there was nothing he could do to change them.

"Just a minute," Sam said. He rose and staggered to the bathroom. Will looked out the window into the black night, listening to Sam retching, and water running. Then he turned down the covers of the bed, and when Sam came out of the bathroom, he helped him remove his boot and worked his pants off over the cast.

"I'm sorry," Sam mumbled.

"It's okay. Lie down." Will covered him and went out, shutting the door behind him. He gathered the empty bottles and put them in the trash. Then he picked up the pieces of broken glass and threw them away. He turned the heat down and went to the door, gazing back into the room. It looked as it always did, neat and calm and orderly.

Outside, the night was cold and remote and wild with stars.

18

Will worked through the long hours of Saturday and Sunday wondering if he should call Sam to check on him. He knew what Mike would do. Not only would she call him, she'd probably have spent the night on the couch, wide awake, listening for trouble. He just hoped she hadn't taken it upon herself to go by there in spite of Sam's wishes. He knew he shouldn't have either, but somehow he wasn't sorry. Sam had needed what he had to offer, Will was now sure of that, and he didn't think Mike, for all her good intentions, could have given the same kind of reserved, almost wordless, solace he'd found in himself to give. Sometimes a man needed another man.

But Will didn't call. His instinct told him not to, and he listened. And in spite of his worry, he was flattered beyond expression that Sam, who'd kept his secret so well from everyone, had told him. He knew it was his secret now, too.

On Monday, as they got into the VW after school, Mike said to him, "Don't you think we should drop in on Sam? See how he's doing?"

"You know he said he'd call when he wanted company." He wasn't about to tell her he'd been there Friday night.

"I know, I know, but what if he didn't really mean it?"

"Mike," he said, warning in his voice.

"What? Oh, all right." She started the car. "So, you want to go straight home?"

"I thought we were going out to your mother's dig."

"Why? She won't be there. She had to go to some meeting in L.A. for three days. She left this afternoon."

"Perfect. You can film without her interfering."

She stared at the road and said nothing.

"You did tell her you'd do it, didn't you?"

"Yeah." She kept her eyes on the road.

"And she gave you back the camera?"

She nodded.

"And film?"

She nodded again.

"Well?"

"I don't want to."

"For God's sake, Mike. What difference does that make? You said you would, and you have to. If you want her to stop treating you like a child, stop acting like one."

She glared at him, and looked back at the road.

"I said I'd help you."

She looked at him again and sighed. "Okay, okay."

He was actually surprised. Paige, the only other person he'd ever tried to persuade, was never at all responsive. He'd quit expecting that.

"Okay, then," he said cheerfully. "Where is it?"

"Out by Little Fish Wash."

They drove past Agua Seca for about eighteen miles, the only sentient life Will knew about in the acres and acres of still sand and scrubby brush. For several miles they'd even been off the highway, following an almost imperceptible track made by Marcella Macey's four-wheel-drive vehicle. Finally Mike braked at the base of some folded mountains which had an opening between them big enough to drive a tank through.

"This is where she's working, at the head of Little Fish Wash where it comes out from between these mountains."

"Little Fish Wash?" he asked, getting out of the car. "Where's the fish? There's nothing but sand and cactus here."

"I can see I'll have to give you a small lecture," Mike said, leaning against the front fender. "Once upon a time, and don't ask me how many zillions of years ago because only Marcella knows, this whole area was covered by sea."

"Really?" Will said, listening more attentively.

"Yes, indeed. Here and there, there are still whole reefs of shells sticking out of the desert, and fish fossils, and sandstone formations marked by wave action. Remarkable but true. And apparently the earliest Indians lived around the edges of this sea. As time went on, for various climatological and archaeological and mysterious reasons, the sea began to shrink, and the Indians followed it as it receded, until there was nothing left. Of the sea, and hardly of the Indians.

"Apparently, a sluggish little stream remained, coming through this split in the mountains and filling some big potholes in the wash. There were fish in the potholes, until a flood came through, erasing the potholes and neatly taking away the fish, too. Not a very hospitable spot for anything. Even the stream dried up after a while.

"Try to imagine what it must have been like, living here. It's bad enough now, with modern conveniences. These poor Indians, the Diegueños, were pretty primitive, as you'd expect, and they haven't left much behind—a few scraps of crude pottery, a few arrowheads, a few bone fragments, some charcoal from old fires.

"During the Second World War, the Navy used this area for a bombing range, and supposedly there are still unexploded bombs around. The ones that exploded took care of some of the Indian artifacts. Don't ask me why the Navy was here. It'd be pretty hard to get a battleship in, but I'm only telling you what was told to me.

"Anyway, Marcella's located an ancient Indian village here at the head of the wash, and she thinks she's found some evidence that they dammed up water behind a rock dike and that, before a huge earthquake caused the water supply to disappear, the Indians used that water for agricultural purposes.

"Please try to contain your excitement while I tell you why this is such a big deal. Most anthropologists and archaeologists and some other kinds of ologists believe that the Indians around here were semi-nomadic hunters and gatherers, following their food supply, and they didn't know diddly-squat about agriculture. Since Marcella found out about this dike thing, and also found some ollas—those are pottery jars, in case you didn't know—full of ironwood seeds in a cave up there somewhere, she thinks they knew how to grow things. Ironwood grows all over here, and I don't know why she thinks the seeds were for planting instead of for eating, but she does.

"So that's it. She's going to knock the scientific community on its ear by trying to prove these wandering seed-gatherers were really farmers. I have no idea why that would make any difference to anybody, but what do I know. So let's go film some of this sand, and watch where you put your feet. Remember those unexploded bombs."

"This was really an ocean once?" Will asked.

Mike rolled her eyes. "Is that where I lost you? I'm not repeating the whole thing."

"I heard the rest," Will said, following her up the wash. "I just thought the part about the ocean was the most interesting."

"Marcella will be overjoyed to hear that."

Will spent the next hour following Mike as she roamed, taking long, sweeping shots of the wash and its surroundings and tight close-ups of the desert vegetation, and strolling into the split between the mountains to look for a cave full of petroglyphs Marcella had found. They couldn't locate it.

"Next time," Mike said. "For now, I'm trying to give an Indian-eye view of what living here must have been like." She turned her camera to the top of the mountain, where the sun rested, waiting to set. "Watching the dark come must have been scary. What a miracle fire must have seemed." She turned the camera onto the shadows lengthening as the sun descended. "Tomorrow let's bring some firewood and get some after-dark pictures. Re-create what it must have been like to live here way back then."

The next night they sat in folding beach chairs in the dark, feeding a small fire and waiting for the full moon to rise so Mike could film it. The fire's orange-and-blue glow was almost lost in the black night.

"Creepy, huh?" Mike said.

"Very. Feels dangerous."

"You want to wait in the car?" she asked. "You'd better say no, because I'm not sitting out here by myself."

"Then no, I guess. Why did you ask?"

"Bravery test. You pass, but just barely."

"Why are we doing this?"

"Filmic verisimilitude."

"In English."

"To make it seem real on film."

"I don't get it. First you don't want to do this at all. Then you don't want to do just the basic job that your mother wants done. And then you're willing to scare us both to death and endanger our lives so something that isn't even necessary looks real."

"If my name's going on this project, I want it to be the best I can do. Someday when I'm famous, somebody might unearth this film and I want it to look good, not slapped together. If I'm going to do it at all, I'm going to do it right. And that means doing it my way, not hers. What does she know about making movies?"

"I don't see how you can say you don't know how to be. You're doing it." He threw a couple of small sticks on the fire.

"What am I doing?"

"You're being what you are. Dedicated, uncompromising, creative, professional. That's a lot for somebody who says she doesn't know what to be. It's more than I know how to be."

"Yeah?" The campfire lit her pleased face. "I like that.

Except for the uncompromising part. That doesn't sound so good, but it's probably true. Well, you're being, too. You're responsible, a real solid citizen. You're loyal, kind, trustworthy, hardworking, and clean in thought, word, and deed."

"Sounds boring as hell," he said glumly.

"It's not. It's rare and wonderful." Her face was pink in the firelight, and she made an embarrassed, dismissive movement of her hand. Then she looked at him again. "What's more, you're really talented at carving. I can tell. Of course, I take some credit, for training your eye."

"You think I'm talented?"

"It's obvious. Anybody could see it. Every one of those animals you do has gotten better than the last one."

"They have? You think they're good?"

"Quit fishing. You know I do."

They sat then, smiling into the fire, pleased with each other and with themselves, waiting for the huge, pale moon to rise and wash them with her ancient light.

19

Just before eight on Saturday night the next weekend, Timothy came in to whisk Paige away from the nuisances of closing. As always, when she saw him, Paige became giddy and aware of herself, tossing her hair over her shoulder too often, laughing too much, watching Timothy through wide eyes as he sat at the counter smiling to himself and folding napkins into origami shapes as he waited for her.

As weird as Will thought Timothy was, he still found him engaging. There seemed to be a sort of gilded envelope of tranquillity around him that affected anybody who came within its radius. Will had seen him break up a fight in the Snakebite on a Saturday afternoon, between two off-roaders who'd had too much beer and too much sun, merely by standing between them and saying, "Be cool. There's too much heat around here already." Much of what he said seemed to have more than one meaning.

Even Paige's giddiness had an innocent, almost childlike quality to it that she had only with Timothy.

"Hi, T.," Will said. "Can I get you some coffee? Oops. I forgot. Juice? Water?"

"Nothing, thanks, Will. I'm just waiting for your radiant sister."

"What you got planned for tonight, T.? Holistic health lecture? A little New Age music? Some crystal gazing?"

Timothy smiled serenely. "Be careful about scoffing at something you don't understand. It could turn back on you."

"Just joking," Will said. Timothy's certainty always made Will wonder if he might not be right, and Will wasn't sure enough about anything to take chances. "Don't turn anything back on me you'll be sorry for."

"It's not up to me, Will. Spirit forces operate on their own."

"Then I hope they've got a sense of humor. Did you hear me, Spirits? Just kidding."

"Paige has learned fast, but I don't think she's passed much of it on to you."

"Paige is a great starter."

"Eventually, one starts the last exploration. One finds what one wants."

"Let's just wait and see with Paige. God knows, I'll be the first one to celebrate if this is her last exploration."

Paige turned the sign to CLOSED, and came to stand by Timothy's stool. "Hi," she said.

"Pretty Paige." He combed his fingers through the hair on either side of her face and held her head between his palms as he kissed her lightly. She closed her eyes. "The night belongs to you and me."

She opened her eyes and gazed into Timothy's smiling face.

"So let us enter into it," he said, taking her hand and leading her out the back door.

The whole exchange made Will want to gag, and he felt even more like it when he realized she'd left him with a sinkload of dirty dishes, all the dirty tables to clear, and everything to get ready for the next morning. He was turning to go after her when Mike came in the back door.

"I saw the CLOSED sign, but I knew you'd still be here. I figured if I helped you we could get out of here quicker."

"What for?"

"We're going over to Sam's. I'm worried about him."

"He hasn't called." Will still hadn't told Mike about his visit to Sam last weekend. Neither had he mentioned that he'd called once and, like a coward, hung up when he heard Sam's slurred voice answer.

After school on Wednesday, they'd driven out to the house site on the way to Little Fish Wash. The roofless building looked forlorn under the glare of the sun. Or maybe it was Will, projecting his own feelings onto the house.

"I don't care," Mike said.

"He said he wanted to be left alone. Some people are like that, you know, when they don't feel right." He knew he was trying to prepare himself for being with Sam again, and he didn't know how long that would take. Sam was different to him now, more vulnerable, sadder, less perfect. And more valuable, for he had shown Will how a good man bears a great sorrow: with painful dignity, which sometimes lapses.

"Oh, in a pig's eye," Mike said. "People only say that because they're afraid of bothering their friends. Well, what are friends for? Just the good times?"

"Yeah. At least, that's the way I've always seen it."

She flicked at him with a towel. Then she turned her back to him and began loading the dishwasher. "I have a confession to make. I was over there this morning. He let me come in, but he was just sitting on the couch with the blinds still pulled shut, and he hardly said two words. And the place was a mess and smelled gicky besides."

"Mike! You shouldn't have done that."

"This is serious, Will." She lowered her voice. "I think he'd been drinking. And it was ten-thirty in the morning. You know he always says he stops after one beer."

"Can't we just let him ride it out? Wait until he feels better and takes a shower and cleans house? I don't want to go."

She turned to face him. "I know that. I don't want to, either. I'm not sure what to do for him. But don't you see? That's what we have to do. Unless he throws us out, and I don't think he will."

"I wish you didn't make it sound so simple and so complicated all at the same time."

"Well, that's how it is. And I can't do it by myself. You have to go with me."

He thought there actually wasn't much Mike couldn't do by herself, but he had to admit he found the prospect of seeing Sam again less daunting when he knew he could share it with Mike. "Oh, all right." He jumped up and down and flapped his hands in front of him and scrunched his face up, while Mike giggled.

When he stopped, she said, "I know. A good tantrum always cheers me up, too. I'll have to teach you how to throw yourself down on your stomach and kick and hold your breath until you pass out."

"I can see I'm dealing with a pro here. Now I'm embarrassed you saw my puny effort."

"You have definite possibilities, for an amateur. Now let's get to work, unless we want to be here all night."

Mike drove them to Sam's, since Timothy and Paige had taken Paige's car. With the heater and the stereo at full blast, the inside of the VW seemed cozy and safe.

Lights blazed through lowered shades from every window of Sam's trailer.

"I guess he hasn't gone to bed," Will said.

"You were hoping he had, weren't you?"

"Absolutely. I could have left a note and run off like the coward I am."

She parked and turned everything off. "You can sit out here and freeze, or come in with me."

"What'll you do for me if I come with you?"

"Allow you to continue living. Come on." She opened the car door.

Mike knocked, waited, and was about to knock again when they heard Sam call, "Who is it?"

"It's Mike and Will. Can we come in?"

"Suit yourself."

Mike opened the door. Sam sat on the couch in the brightly lit, disorderly room, a misshapen chunk of wood on an open newspaper on the coffee table. There were empty bottles on the table, too, and drifts of newspapers around the couch. Clothing led in a trail to the bedroom door as if he had undressed on his way to the tumbled bed they could see through the open door.

Sam leaned back on the couch, a beer bottle balanced on his stomach. The chunk of wood had been worked on with a whittling knife, but it looked as if it had been attacked rather than formed.

Mike and Will looked at each other, and Will lifted his shoulders fractionally.

"Have you had any dinner?" Mike asked briskly.

Sam frowned. "Can't remember."

She went to the couch and took the beer bottle out of his hand. "It's not good for you to drink on an empty stomach. It'll make you sick. Let me fix you a sandwich and then you can have this back if you want." She held the neck of the bottle between her thumb and forefinger as if she could hardly prevent herself from wrinkling her nose.

"Okay," Sam said, meek as a child.

Mike carried the bottle to the kitchen, and though Will wanted to follow her, he sat down in the chair opposite Sam. Gesturing to the wood chunk, he said, "Starting something new?"

"I couldn't do it." He looked at Will with watery eyes.

"What was it going to be?"

"A soldier. The head of a soldier. I couldn't do it."

"Oh." Will knew Sam's talent was equal to the job. Was he trying to carve Kevin? "Why don't you try to make something else, then?"

Sam leaned his head back on the couch and closed his eyes.

Will picked up the wood and the knife and began to work on it. He could see the vague shape of a head, but he knew it was beyond his ability to bring it out. Sam had told him that one miscarve could ruin a whole piece, or you could go with the scar and make it into something else. Maybe not something better, but something different. It was the carver's choice.

Will decided to shape the wood into Mike's VW. He'd try to make a string of musical notes oozing out the window and streaming along the side of the car. Maybe he could carve a little figure of Mike to go inside the car. Maybe he could put himself in there, too.

He concentrated on the carving, and when Mike came back in with the sandwich, he looked up guiltily. He was supposed to be doing something about Sam, and here he was, working on his own project. But he hadn't known what else to do.

Mike put the sandwich plate on Sam's lap and sat down next to him. "Eat that."

Sam obediently picked up the sandwich and took a bite. "What is it?" he asked.

"Weasel. Just eat it."

"Huh," Sam said. "I thought I'd used up all the weasel."

Mike giggled, and Will felt as relieved as she sounded. A joke was a good sign.

Mike watched Sam eat, and Will could see the muscles in her jaw flex as Sam chewed. When he finished, she took the plate and sat up straighter next to him. She cleared her throat, and Will braced himself. He knew she was preparing for one of her characteristic head-on collisions.

"Sam," she began.

He held up his hand to her. "I know. You don't need to give me a lecture."

"I wasn't going to." Sam's expression was skeptical. "You're scaring me, is all."

"Don't worry about me, Mike. I've survived more than a few of these moods. I expect I'll survive one more."

"But why?" she asked.

Will cracked his knuckles, and she gave him a sharp

look. He stopped, and picked up the wooden VW again.

"Old ghosts, honey. None of your concern."

"I'm your friend. I want to help," she said.

He smiled and patted her hand, more like the old Sam, and not the unfamiliar man he'd seemed when they first arrived.

"Thanks for that. And that's a big help right there."

"In other words, it's none of my business."

"Yep."

Will knew, though, and their shared secret filled him with pride.

"Well, okay," she said. "As long as you promise you'll shape up and quit worrying me."

"You sound like somebody's mother," Sam said.

"Oh, God," Mike said, clapping her hands to her cheeks. "I sound just like mine. Forget I said that. You just go on doing whatever you want. Bring all the disgrace on the family you want to. Don't give a single thought to how much you'll be breaking my heart." She covered her mouth. "I can't stop."

"Wouldn't Marcella be pleased," Sam said.

"Arghhh," Mike said, falling back on the couch. "The last thing in the world I want to do."

Sam stood up. "I'm going to bed. It seems to be the only way I can get away from your unnecessary solicitude. You can go ahead and pour that beer down the sink."

Mike stood up, too. "I already did. You want me to tuck you in?"

"Go home, you two. Or go do something fun. Don't let an old man reliving old miseries get in your way. They'll pass. Just turn out the lights and lock up when you leave." He went into his bedroom and shut the door.

Mike went around turning off lights. "Let's go."

In the car Mike said, "Now, aren't you glad I made you go? We helped him. He ate and he's getting some rest and I poured out the beer. We turned him around."

"Maybe," Will said. "Or maybe he was ready to do it himself." He knew, from his mother's death, that anniversaries of grief have their own limits.

"Well, I'm going to take some credit, whether you want to or not. By the way, I don't think it was very nice of you to take away his carving. He'd just started it."

"He didn't want it," Will said. "It wasn't helping."

"What do you think he's hiding from us? Something about his wife?"

"I don't know," Will said, looking out the window.

For the next two weeks, except on Fridays, when Will had to work, Mike and Will stopped at Sam's after school, just as they might have gone to the adobe site. Once Mike was sure that Sam was through his crisis, she took advantage of the break from construction to work on her mother's video. After a brief visit with Sam, she'd leave to throw her abundant energy into her new project, typically unable to go halfway once she'd committed herself.

After she'd gone, Sam and Will would settle down to whittle in companionable silence, making Sam's one beer and Will's Coke last the whole afternoon. Sometimes Will stayed to dinner, other times he went back to the Snakebite, leaving Sam his privacy. He couldn't say how he sensed which choice was appropriate on which night, but Sam never asked him to stay on nights when he knew to go.

Only later did Will realize that his eighteenth birthday had passed without his notice while he was preoccupied with Sam. He no longer needed Paige as his guardian. Somehow, he'd thought he would feel free at eighteen, but he felt no different at all.

20

One morning, on the way to school, Mike yelled to Will over the Mozart, "Okay, brace yourself, big boy."

"For what?"

"My mother wants to meet you. She wants to know who this guy is I'm spending so much time with; are you acceptable to her discriminating requirements. So she wants you to have dinner with us tonight."

"Well, I have been curious about what you eat if you don't eat dead things."

"I won't even give you a hint. If you knew about tofu, you'd never come."

"Could that have been a hint and I'm just too dumb to know it?"

"Don't you bother your pretty little head about it. I'll pick you up at six. Bone up on your table manners. There'll be a test."

Paige sat on the sagging couch, painting her nails, her feet up on the coffee table, when Will came out of his bedroom dressed in khakis, a shirt, and a sweater, his hair brushed.

"Wow," she said. "Somehow I don't think you're going to spend the evening watching TV with me."

"I'm having dinner at Mike's."

"Going to meet the family?"

"Not the way you think. How come you're staying home tonight? Aren't you entering into the night with Timothy?"

She smeared nail polish on her thumb. "Damn!" She wiped at the smudge with a tissue. "I believe he'll be entering into it with someone else tonight. Her name's Cindy Naughton, I hear."

"What?" He could hardly imagine a less likely combination. "I thought you two were a tight item."

Intently examining her nails, she said, "So did I."

Will sat down next to her. "When did this happen?"

"A few days ago."

"Are you okay about it?"

"No." She stuck the brush back in the bottle and lit a cigarette.

He bit back a remark. It was the first cigarette he'd seen her smoke since they came to the desert. "So it wasn't your idea?"

"Very perceptive. He decided he needed some space. He doesn't want to feel weighted. He wants to go to San Francisco and work for animal rights."

"When?"

"Soon. He's planning. Loosening his ties. Lightening his attachments. Maintaining his flexibility—and other crap like that."

"I'm sorry, Paige. He was . . . interesting."

"I thought so, too." She flopped back on the couch, waving her wet nails. "Now what am I going to do in this godforsaken place?"

"What about all that opening to a new experience,

exploring a new side of yourself, getting in tune with your inner workings? Buying a dune buggy?" He knew it was unkind as soon as he said it; he couldn't seem to help it. At least, Timothy had kept her occupied. What kind of mischief would she find without him?

She gave him a murderous look. "Shut up."

He stood. "Truline doesn't think this is a godforsaken place."

"Why don't you go to your dinner party and leave me alone?"

"Good idea. I'll wait for Mike outside." There had been light rain that day, and the desert air was clean, with the tang of sage. He realized he'd almost forgotten what the ocean smelled like. He was only two hours away from it, but the barrier of the mountains and the enveloping vastness of the desert made it seem a figment of his imagination.

Mike's headlights caught him as she came tearing up the road, and she braked beside him.

"Very nice," she said, surveying him as he got into the car.

"Thanks. You, too. I've never seen you in a skirt before."

She gave an embarrassed shrug. "Marcella's laying on the linen and the good china."

"I'll try not to blow my nose on the tablecloth. I was hoping it'd be more of a paper plates and plastic forks kind of deal."

"Not Marcella's style. Even on a remote exploration, she brings a crate of china and silver and enough Vouvray to last the whole trip."

"What's Vouvray? Anything like tofu?"

"Fortunately not. It's wine. The amenities count big with her. Do it right or don't do it at all is her motto. And doing it right means doing it her way."

"Where have I heard that before? Maybe you two have something in common, after all."

"It's different when I say it."

"Whatever you say. I sure am looking forward to this evening. Can't you tell her I've got a headache and had to take to my bed?"

"Chicken. I've got to live with her every day. You can stand one night. I thought you were strong like bull."

They pulled up in front of a big white double trailer.

"The lion's den?" Will asked.

"She takes it with her everywhere she can. Home on wheels."

Mike opened the door, and Will followed her into a large square room furnished mostly in shades of gray. The color in the decor came from artifacts artfully displayed on walls and tabletops: pots and sculptures, framed shards and what looked like war clubs, a stone embedded with fossils. The lighting was low and peaceful, and if he didn't know better, Will might have thought he was in a high-rise city apartment. At one end of the room, a table was set with a pale pink cloth and glittering dinnerware.

Marcella Macey came into the room from the kitchen. "You must be Will," she said, extending her hand. She was tall and slender, her auburn hair gathered into a loose roll at the back of her neck. Her skirt was flowered in pink and gray, and she wore a thin pink sweater. Will wondered if she'd dressed to match the room. He never would have guessed that she and Mike were related.

"It's nice to meet you, Mrs., I mean, Dr. Macey."

"Call me Marcella." Quiet authority was in her voice.

Mike turned so that Will could see her face but her mother couldn't, and rolled her eyes up in her head.

"Pretty place," he said.

"I like to have somewhere nice to come to after a day spent grubbing around. Sit down. Can I get you something to drink? A glass of wine?"

"Have you got any Vouvray?"

"Vouvray?" She shot a look at Mike, who was looking elsewhere. "In fact, I do. Mike?"

"No, thanks. I'll get myself a root beer."

"As long as you're going to the kitchen, why don't you bring Will's wine? And a glass for me as well."

"Right." Mike's retreating back was rigid.

Marcella Macey sat on the couch with Will. "Now tell me what a young Vouvray fancier like you is doing living here."

"It was my sister's idea. To try something different."

"You're a risk-taker, then?"

"Uh—" He didn't think he'd call himself that, but look at where he was. It felt risky, all right. "Maybe. A little."

"And how are you finding it?"

"Okay, I guess."

She watched him attentively, as if he were an especially interesting artifact.

"Come now. I'd like to know."

Mike came back with two glasses of wine, which she set down on the coffee table with such a thud that Will's spilled a little.

"Really, Mike," her mother said mildly. "Bring Will another glass."

Mike turned and stalked back to the kitchen.

Dr. Macey shook her head slightly and raised her fine eyebrows, giving Will a conspiratorial look. "About the desert?" she prompted.

"It's not what I expected."

"And what did you expect?"

"Sand dunes and nothing else. I was surprised there's so much vegetation and so many animals. And so much sky and silence."

"Yes," she said, nodding approvingly. "Wild places all have silence, filled with echoes."

"I guess you can hear the echoes better than I can."

"That's why I'm an anthropologist."

Mike returned with her root beer and Will's wine. Marcella seemed deaf to the echoes Mike was broadcasting.

"Thank you, dear," Marcella said.

Mike dropped into an armchair of gray suede and chrome.

"I've been out to where you're working."

"Really? With Mike?" She looked at Mike and her eyes opened wider as Mike stared into her root beer. "And how is the project coming along?"

Mike gave a shrug that could have meant anything.

"Well," Marcella said, looking triumphant. Turning back to Will, she said, "I'm giving a paper at the end of April at a very important meeting. I think I have something exciting to report, and a video record would make it that much more exciting. Mike's been rather, ah, reluctant to cooperate, but I think things will work out."

"She told me about your Indian agriculture theory," Will said.

"Did she?" Once again, Marcella looked surprised. "It's so difficult to tell when she's listening."

Then she went on talking about her career to Will as if he were her equal in age, education, and professional status. She addressed nothing to Mike, who, presumably, had heard it all before, and Mike contributed nothing except a few loud slurps on her root beer.

"Excuse me. I need to check on dinner," Dr. Macey said, and went into the kitchen.

Will turned to Mike and whispered, "Does she think I'm the president of Harvard or something?"

"She's making you feel like that, isn't she? Marcella's irresistible in high gear." Mike sounded both sad and disgusted.

Will couldn't deny he was flattered by Marcella's focus on him, but also baffled by it. "I'm just a kid," he told Mike.

"Don't I know it. She could just be practicing her charm, keeping it from rusting out here in Sand Land. Maybe she's demonstrating to me what a fabulous role model she is, and how little I've taken advantage of it. Maybe she has the hots for your bod, like Cindy did."

"That's probably it."

Dr. Macey came in carrying a crystal salad bowl, which she put on the table. "Mike, please bring the stuffed squash and we can eat."

The dinner-table conversation was dominated by Dr. Macey talking about her work. Will couldn't deny it was fascinating, and after a while he was quite caught up in the exotic quality of what she talked about: the sex practices of Trobriand Islanders, Bantu burial practices,

Manus kinship systems. How could Mike not find this interesting? Especially when she said that what she wanted from college was to learn about things she'd never heard of before. This evening with Marcella had given him an idea of what he would miss by not going to college.

The only word Mike spoke during dinner was in response to his question about what the squash was stuffed with.

"Tofu," she said, and didn't elaborate.

When the dishes had been cleared and the coffee and fruit tart served, Marcella said, "Please forgive me. I get carried away when I talk about my work."

"I enjoyed it," Will said. That sounded lame, he knew, but it was all he could think of. He felt too ignorant to try to say more.

Mike stirred three spoonsful of sugar into her coffee cup and still made a face when she sipped it.

"Now, Will," Marcella said, patting her lips with a napkin, "you must tell me what you've discovered since you came to live in the desert."

So he told her about the adobe house and his new interest in wood carving. He didn't even try to put into words what he had learned about friendship, from Mike and from Sam; about doing and being, and growing into a man.

"And your sister, what is her interest in the desert?"

"That's a good question. She's just restless. She likes to try new things—for a while."

"Every new experience leaves its mark. She'll be changed by having been here."

"Paige seems to be able to stay the same, no matter where she is. She's more likely to change the place than to have it change her."

Marcella laughed lightly. "Changing *this* place is beyond her abilities, I think. I find it a much more attractive quality to be adaptive, to learn from where you are. Especially from a place like the desert, which evokes such passion. I'm passionate about my own concerns and I like being around people who are equally passionate about theirs."

"Sam's that way, about his house," Will said.

"I find him a sad person."

"Sam? Why?"

"He's passionate only about creating a hiding place. It'll doubtless be a magnificent hiding place, but a hiding place nonetheless."

"It's his choice," Will said defensively, even though he suspected what she said was true.

"Indeed. And a wrong one for a man of Sam's talents."

"Maybe he'll be one to change something here."

"Perhaps." She turned to Mike. "And perhaps someday something about this severe and challenging environment will encourage you to develop your own passions."

Mike only looked levelly at her mother, while Will's mouth opened to comment on Mike's video work. She was as passionate about that as should be allowed by law. How could Dr. Macey have missed it?

Mike turned her cold gaze on Will and he shut his mouth.

21

As she drove him home, Mozart loud and bright around them, he yelled, "Doesn't she know how much you love to make movies?"

Mike gave him the same cold look.

He yelled, "I said—" He reached out and shut off the music. "Why do I get the feeling you're mad at me? What was I supposed to do?"

"You were a perfect guest. You hung on her every word and were excruciatingly polite."

"I realize that's a concept foreign to you, but so what? That's just good manners. Besides, what she talked about was interesting."

"She thinks she knows everything. She doesn't even know I like to make movies."

"You mean, you keep it a secret on purpose?"

"She's so self-centered, she thinks one of the reasons I didn't want to film her dig—besides the fact that I'm naturally stubborn and uncooperative, of course—was because I couldn't get interested in using the camera. Does that sound like somebody who's paying attention?"

"What do you want her to do?"

"Just once, I'd like her to give me the kind of one-on-one she gave you over dinner. All that junk about what do you like to do and what are you passionate about."

Mike did a perfect imitation of her mother, to the point of gazing so intently into his face that he was afraid she'd drive right off the road.

"Watch it!"

She straightened the wheel.

"But you always say she talks to you all the time."

"She talks *at* me. She's always instructing or lecturing or reproaching me. She talks, but she never listens."

"Maybe you'll never get what you want from her," he said. "Have you ever thought about that?"

"Yes. I think about it all the time." Tears shone on her cheeks in the dash lights. She rubbed a hand over her face and the car leaped, accelerating down the dark road.

"Pull over," Will said, putting his hand on the wheel. "You can't drive like this. Come on."

The car slowed and came to a stop on the shoulder. Will turned the key in the ignition, and Mike put her head down on her arms crossed over the steering wheel. "What's wrong with me?" She sobbed. "Why can't she love me?"

He raised his hand, hesitated, and slowly brought it down on her narrow back. He rubbed up and down, feeling the knobs of her spine. "Maybe it's her, not you."

"It can't be her." Mike's voice was muffled. "She's perfect. I'm just me. Too odd and difficult. And I can't be any other way."

"You don't have to be any other way. You're fine. You're just different from her, that's all." He didn't think it was the right time to point out to her the similarities he saw between her and Marcella: the strength and spirit and dedication to what they cared about. The fact that they cared about different things was their main difference. She was silent, so he went on. "She doesn't know you. I do. I know what you like to do and what you're passionate about. So does Sam. We know you're odd and difficult. That's what we like about you. That's what makes you be you. Don't we count?" He continued to rub her bony back.

"I can be such a witch," she said in a choked voice.

"So? You're my best friend, too." Those words were the truth.

She lifted her head. In the starry glow, Will could see that her eyes were swollen and her nose was running. "I am?"

"I've talked to you about stuff nobody else knows. And you've listened and understood."

There was a long, thoughtful silence.

"Have you got a tissue?" she asked.

"No. You want to use my shirt?"

"Don't be disgusting. I'll use mine." She pulled the tail of her blouse out and wiped her eyes and nose on it. "I'm a mess."

"You sure are. Are you through being goofy?"

"I probably won't ever be through, but I'm done for the moment." She started the car and eased back onto the road. They were quiet all the way to the Snakebite.

Will wasn't sure if he regretted what he'd told her, but it was too late now. And besides, she *was* his best friend. Nobody'd ever paid the kind of attention to him that she had, or helped him think about so many things. She'd gradually chipped away at the fear he had of getting involved with someone else's life, shown him it wasn't so scary; that it could be rewarding even when it was scary, the way it had been that night around the campfire at Little Fish Wash; the way it had been the night he found Sam drunk and grieving. The part that took away the fear was knowing that another person was in it with him, to respond, to share, to have fun with: the things Paige did so little of.

When she let him off in front of the Snakebite, all she said was, "Good night. See you in the morning." But he knew she meant more.

Paige's car was gone, he noticed, as he unlocked the trailer door.

He turned on the living-room lights, thinking, I hope she's not out doing something stupid. The ashtray on the coffee table was full of crushed cigarette butts and there were several partly full cups of coffee on the table, too.

He turned off the lights and was in the bathroom brushing his teeth when he heard her car pull up. She was smiling when she came to lean against the bathroom door holding a book against her chest.

"Where were you?" he asked, his mouth full of toothpaste.

"You gave me a good idea, little brother."

"What do you mean?"

"When you said Truline didn't think this was a god-forsaken place."

"Yeah?" he asked cautiously.

"I went to see her. She always seems so happy and at peace. I thought maybe she could help."

"And?"

"And she did. She showed me I need Someone bigger than myself to depend on. That if I have faith, I'll have what I want. 'Ask and it will be given you; seek and you will find; knock and it will be opened to you.' That's Matthew 7:7," she said proudly.

Will rinsed his mouth. "You've been with Truline all this time?"

She nodded. "She taught me to pray. I can't tell you the serenity I feel, the quiet within my soul. Thank you." She stood on tiptoe and kissed his cheek. "God bless you."

She went into her room and closed the door, still holding the brand-new Bible against her chest.

Great, Will thought, throwing himself into bed. And it had been his idea for her to go to Truline. He sat up. No, it hadn't. All he'd said was that Truline didn't think this was a godforsaken place. Paige had made her own choice, as she always did. He didn't know why he bothered to say anything at all to her. It never made any difference.

He lay down again. It wasn't the same with Mike. What he said went inside her head. He could almost see the process of his words being whirled around in some kind of complicated machinery inside Mike's skull; having the juice and meaning extracted, combining that with some idea of her own that was already there. The new product was an amalgam of his thought and hers, something new the two of them had produced together.

With Paige, his words went in and hit a long slippery slide, the kind he still loved to find in swimming pools. They hit that slide, fell into the water, and sank out of sight, never to be seen again.

22

As soon as Sam's foot was out of the cast, he rented a skip-loader to hoist the vigas to the roof, and he, Will, and Mike were back in the house-building business.

As they got ready to raise the viga that would run across the middle of the living-room ceiling, Will noticed it still had FIFI AND HIS KIDS, WIL AND MYK written on it in yellow chalk.

"Don't you want to wash that chalk off first?" Will asked Sam.

"Naw. Leave it. I kind of like the way it looks."

So it went up as it was.

For the next month, they were able to work on the house almost every day. The only interruptions were a few days of light rain, which resulted in a quick burgeoning of tiny wildflowers scattered across the desert floor. The ocotillo, with its mouse-eared leaves, burst into brilliant scarlet bloom at its tips, and even the homely creosote bushes sported yellow blossoms.

To Will's eye, the barrenness had come to life. Thunderheads piled over the mountains gave dimension to a sky that for so long had been relentlessly blank and blue.

Even the showers that evaporated before they reached the ground were a welcome diversion.

The days were hotter now, at the end of March, and the afternoons longer. Though Will used lots of sunblock, working shirtless he was gradually getting a tan even the most ardent beach bum would envy. His biceps improved, too, as he muscled the house toward completion.

He liked to stand on the top of the house, resting from laying the cedros in their herringbone pattern, and look out across the dry, empty miles at the heat shimmers in the distance, imagining they were the reflection of the great sea that had once been there. He inhaled the dehydrated air, breathing in the perfume of mesquite and sage, and thought he could smell water.

He could hardly believe it, but he was happy.

He didn't expect that feeling would last, but he was going to enjoy it while he had it. Paige seemed settled, for the moment, in the comfort of Truline and her Bible studies, Timothy resolutely put from her mind, even though he hadn't left Agua Seca yet, and even continued to come into the Snakebite. Sam was back to drinking one beer a day, spending all his daylight hours at the house and doing his carvings at night, often with Will, the way he'd done before he broke his foot.

Mike had been busy for the past week, putting the finishing touches on Marcella's video, and hadn't stayed at the house site after school, though she dropped Will off and paused long enough to admire the progress. The way Will and Sam worked together without her was different:

quieter, more deliberate, more . . . more masculine, was the only way Will could think to describe it. He liked it.

He stood on top of the building, gazing off at the distant mountains and the smudges of green marking paloverde, smoke trees, and catalpa, flexing his brown arms and feeling strong and able.

"Look lively," Sam called from the ground. "Here comes a load of insulation."

"You've got some mail," Paige told him when he came into the trailer after school a week later. "I put it in your room."

He had a term paper to write and needed the afternoon to work on it. He'd planned to bag the paper and help Sam anyway, but Mike had told him he'd have to walk to the site if he did that; she wasn't going to contribute to his failing in school by driving him over there.

He couldn't see what difference it made. School grades this late in the senior year were only important if he was going on to college, which he wasn't. Mike reminded him he might want to someday and he'd be sorry if he blew it now. Grumbling, he'd gotten out of the car at the Snakebite and watched enviously as she drove off to meet Sam.

Aside from a couple of postcards from Jay, Will had had no mail since he'd come to Agua Seca. Jay's postcards were singularly uninformative. They said things like "Surf's up and I miss watching you wipe out," or "The service at Pizza on Wheels has improved 100% since you left."

On his pillow was another colorful beach-scene postcard and a long, white envelope. Will turned the card over and read: "San Diego State has been unwise enough to accept me. Will I see you there? Jay."

"Fat chance," Will muttered, examining the white envelope. The return address was UCLA. Probably a recruiting flyer. Mike had been getting letters from all kinds of institutes of higher learning, including Jake Tiano's School of Bartending, and The New Age College of Crystal Healing, just because she was a graduating senior. Will figured his were going to the house in Imperial Beach, if he was getting them at all, and that Chuck was throwing them away.

He tore open the envelope.

Dear Will Griffin:
We are pleased to inform you that you have been accepted for admission to the University of California at Los Angeles.

He dropped the letter. Was it a joke? He hadn't applied to UCLA, or to anyplace else. There must be a trick, like those contests that said, "You may have won $1,000,000," making it sound as if it had already happened.

He picked up the letter and read through it, and if there was a joke, he couldn't find it. The letter told him when to respond by and how to reserve dorm space, and that his financial-aid package would be arriving under separate cover.

He went into the living room and said, "Paige, I've got to take the car. I don't know when I'll be back."

"No problem," she said from where she sat on the couch reading her Bible. "Truline's coming over later and we're not going anywhere." She took a closer look at him. "Bad news?"

"I don't know." He dug her keys out of her purse and took off.

Mike and Sam were at the house, inside, out of the sun, arguing about how many shelves to put in the bookcases as they worked on the curved corner fireplace.

Will's shadow from the doorway fell across them before they noticed him.

"Hi," Mike said. "What are you doing here? I thought you were going to write that paper."

"It'll keep."

"Well, then, tell Sam he needs more shelves for paperbacks than for big books. Everybody owns more paperbacks than—what's wrong?"

"I got a letter from UCLA today."

Mike was still and silent for a moment, but Will saw the quick glance between her and Sam. "So?" she said.

"I've been accepted there. With financial aid."

"That's wonderful!" She started for him, her arms wide, then took another look at his face. "Isn't it?" She dropped her arms.

"I didn't apply to UCLA. I didn't apply anywhere. And I have a hard time believing they've heard about me and took it upon themselves to offer me a place. You two wouldn't know anything about this, would you?"

Mike and Sam looked at each other again. Sam took a step forward, still limping slightly, even though he'd been out of his cast for over a month. "You're the kind of person who should go to college, Will. You'd value it, and you'd profit from it. You should have the chance."

Will stood where he was, the letter in his hand.

"Okay!" Mike burst out. "We submitted your application for you. I confess, I went to the trailer one night when you were at work and swiped it right off your bureau. You never even noticed. And Sam sent a couple of your carvings. He didn't think you'd miss them."

"So that's what happened to my kangaroo rat and my rattlesnake. Why didn't you tell me?" He knew he sounded furious. He was.

"Because we were afraid you'd act just like you're acting now, only now it's too late to do anything but accept. If they don't take me, too, I'm really going to be mad."

"You had no right to do this without telling me."

"I don't see what you're so upset about."

"Come, sit down, and let's talk about this," Sam said.

"We are talking about it, and there's no place to sit."

"What's the deal?" Mike asked. "Don't you want to go?"

"How can I go? What about Paige?"

"What about her?" Mike said. "She's over twenty-one. She can do what she wants to do."

"But she makes terrible choices. She needs somebody to help her."

"Why does it have to be you?" Mike's voice rose. "Why do you have to take the consequences of her terrible choices?"

"Because she's my sister. We're all each other has."

"Oh, bull pucky. I don't know what she's got, but you've got more than her. You've got us. And you'll have a lot more if you go to UCLA. When is she going to grow up? When are *you* going to?"

"You don't know what you're talking about."

"The hell I don't."

"Hey, you two," Sam said, "cut it out. Let's be logical. Now, Will, what'll happen to Paige if you don't go to UCLA?"

"I don't know. I never know what she'll do next. That's why I have to stay loose—to go after her."

"Okay," Sam continued. "What'll happen to her if you *do* go to UCLA?"

"Same answer. Except I won't be there to help her. And the mess she gets herself in will be worse by the time I find out about it."

Mike rolled her eyes and turned her back on Will to bang her head lightly against the fireplace. "Whose mess is it, anyway?"

Sam went on. "You mean she's incapable of cleaning up her own mess?"

"Yes!" Will yelled. "She always has been."

"How come you're so good at it?"

"Because I've had to do it. Why is this so hard for you to understand?"

"How, then, do you suppose Paige could learn to do it?"

"But she won't. She'll just end up wrecking herself."

"Maybe. Maybe not. But she's going to wreck you for sure."

"What's wrong with you two? Don't you see I have no choice?"

"You've almost always got a choice, boy," Sam said.

"Not this time." Will turned and ran back to his car. He felt tears rising and he'd be damned if he'd let them show. Of course, he wanted to go to UCLA. To be able to study whatever he wanted, to concentrate only on himself for four years sounded like Paradise. But the price was too high. He couldn't pay for his education with Paige.

He drove fast along the empty roads, crisscrossing the phantom sea, for a long time before he turned the car back toward the Snakebite. He calmed down enough to know that Mike and Sam had thought they were giving him a generous, unexpected gift, and they were. But they'd also given him the pain of having to reject it.

When he got back to the trailer, Paige and Truline were sitting on the couch, hands clasped together and heads bowed. Truline looked up and said, "Evening, Willie," but Paige stayed in her prayer.

"Sorry. Don't let me disturb you," Will said, making for his room. He fell onto his bed and lay staring at the ceiling. Could he believe that, with Truline's brand of truth, Paige had finally found what she was looking for? Would it really be possible for him to leave her, safe and stable inside her own life, while he went looking for his?

He imagined her in a white gown before a tent full of believers. Paige wouldn't settle for being one of the crowd; she'd have to be out front. He could see her, pure and fiery, like Sister Sharon Falconer in *Elmer Gantry*, his favorite book from his junior-year class in Major American Writers. She could do it if she wanted. He never expected her to have an ordinary life; he just wanted her to have one she controlled herself.

Yeah, and look what happened to Sister Sharon. She fell in love with a con man and burned to death in a fire.

That would never have happened if Will had been around. He'd have figured out a way to save her.

He flopped onto his side. Maybe Paige would be willing to live in Los Angeles with him. He'd give up staying in a dorm and share an apartment with her so he could keep an eye on her. There should be lots of things in L.A. to catch her interest and keep her busy.

Lots of the wrong things. Los Angeles would be too tempting. And who's to say she could stay anywhere for four years ever again, now that she'd had a taste of moving on?

But maybe it would work for a while. Maybe he could get a year there before she got itchy again.

And how would that make him feel? Would he begin to hate her for making him give it up after a year? Was he going to hate her now if he didn't go at all?

It was too hard to ask himself all these questions. He had no answers. He got off the bed and opened his one window. Leaning his elbows on the sill, he stretched his neck out into the wide desert night filled with mystery, and listened to nothing.

And then he heard the coyotes starting up. By now he knew their sounds: the overlapping yips and barks, like confused conversation. Like what was going on in his own head. And then the chorus of howls aimed at the moon. Over and over, long, undulating howls.

He wished he could join them in their song.

By morning, Will was gritty-eyed and heavy-headed from lack of sleep, but he'd made a sort of decision. He'd wait until the last possible day to let UCLA know. It would give him time to watch Paige, to see if being with Truline would calm her enough that he felt secure about leaving her. He might be clutching at straws, hoping for a miracle, but he bet Truline would say that could happen. If anybody needed one, it was him.

23

For the next month, Will watched Paige like a warden.

Any change in her meant changes for him, changes he didn't want. He felt as if he had to hold his breath until the first of May, when he would have to respond to UCLA, and then again until the first of June, when they were to leave for Imperial Beach. He'd give anything to have been able to gleefully send back the response the day he had received the acceptance letter, the way Mike had.

If Paige sensed his watchfulness, she didn't let on. She continued to get up early to read her Bible, to pray with Truline in the afternoons, to be loving and patient with him. She even insisted he leave right at closing on the weekends, while she did the final cleaning, so he could go to Sam's and work on his growing menagerie of carved desert animals.

Will went to school and plastered walls at the adobe. He moved rocks and worked on his animals. And all the time he watched Paige, while Mike and Sam watched him. They didn't mention college to him again, or Paige, but those subjects lay like land mines in their conversations, to be carefully avoided. They all felt the strain.

* * *

Two more days to go.

After he got dressed for school, he licked the envelope with his acceptance of UCLA's offer and sealed it shut. It was already addressed and stamped. He stuck it into his American History book and opened the door to the living room.

Paige was sitting on the couch, showered, dressed, reading her Bible. "Good morning," she said.

"Hi. You're up early again."

"I like it. Everything's nice and quiet."

"It's always quiet around here."

"A good kind of quiet. Peaceful. I've been thinking I might stay through the summer, and work here again in the fall. Maybe I could be a caretaker or something until then."

"Stay here in the summer? I thought you wanted to go back to Imperial Beach."

She shrugged. "I've changed my mind. But I know how you love the beach, and how hard it's been for you to be here. Why don't you go home without me? I'll be fine."

"I can't believe what I'm hearing."

"Well, believe it. I'm happy here. I feel serene. Can't you tell?"

"You do seem different. But you've seemed that way before."

She tapped her Bible. "I never had this before. You know how much I wanted to come here. It must have been instinct. I must have known I'd find something."

Warily, but with rising hope, he said, "Well, great."

He didn't know if this was the right time to tell her, but there might not be a better one. "What would you think if I went to, uh, college in the fall?"

"Oh, Will, I wish you could. But the money . . ."

"What if that wasn't a problem?"

"Well, of course I'd want that for you. It would be wasted on me, but not on you."

"UCLA wants me. On full scholarship."

"Will! Why didn't you tell me?" She closed the Bible.

"I didn't think I'd be going, so what was the point?"

She got up and hugged him. "Go. You have to go."

He hugged her back. "I guess I will, then." Is it really going to be this simple, he wondered. "I've got to get out of here. Mike'll be along any minute."

She let him go. "I'm so proud of you."

He went out the door and ran to the road, leaping into the air every few steps and yelling inarticulate sounds.

He was in midair when Mike stopped for him. He opened the door and yelled into the car, "I'm going to UCLA!"

"Well, thank goodness you've come to your senses. Get in and tell me everything."

All the way to school he yelled over the Mozart, telling Mike about Paige's decision. He'd have been yelling even if there hadn't been any Mozart.

"I thought you said she always made bad choices," Mike said.

"And you said she had to change eventually. She has."

"I don't recall putting it exactly like that, but I don't care what I said, as long as it means we can go to college together."

"I'm mailing this today." He pulled the letter out of his history book. "Before something happens to it."

"I'll help you. Just to be sure."

After school they went by the post office, where Will kissed the letter and dropped it in the slot. Then they drove to the adobe house through the stunning glare of the desert afternoon.

Sam had gone to Calexico for the day to pick up more floor tiles, but it was cool and quiet inside the nearly finished house, and besides, they just liked being there.

"Did Marcella get back yesterday?" Will asked, popping open a Classic Coke and handing Mike a root beer from Sam's cooler. "How did her presentation go?"

They sat on cushions on the smooth tile floor, their backs against the newly plastered wall. "She tried to be so cool about it, like she didn't want me to know how good my work was, but I'd already listened to the messages on her answering machine, so I knew how much everybody liked the video. They all said things like 'Interesting idea about the agriculture. Who made the great video?' " Mike laughed. "That's what they said. The Great Video. And it was, wasn't it?"

"You couldn't have done it without me, remember?" he prompted.

"I couldn't have done it without you. I remember." She sounded absolutely sincere.

"So did she ever tell you it was a Great Video?"

"Are you kidding? Did she ever tell me she was proud of me for getting into UCLA? All she said was it's a shame it wasn't Harvard. She said her presentation went quite well and the audiovisual aid was helpful. Helpful!"

"Forget it," Will said, guzzling his Coke. "You and I know, and soon the world will know. Then let her try to ignore you."

"She'll probably find a way. But it makes me feel better about going to film school. I know I have what it takes."

"I've known it all along."

To Will's amazement, Mike blushed. He clamped his mouth shut, just in case he was tempted to make some smart remark so she wouldn't think he was getting mushy in his old age.

Mike cleared her throat and changed the subject. "Now that I know for sure I'm going to UCLA, I'm getting worried about college social life. These last two years in Sand Land have had a retarding effect on my social skills."

"Yeah. And all you drink is root beer. I guess you'll be spending a lot of time in the library studying."

She poured some root beer on her fingers and flicked them at him. "The best way to meet people in a school as big as UCLA is to get involved in activities. I'd better join the Wallflowers Club."

"Good plan. I'm sure that'll improve your social skills."

"Seriously. I'm going to join as many things as interest me. Even if I don't make any friends, I'll be doing activities I enjoy."

"What makes you think you won't make any friends?"

"The past two years haven't done much to convince me I'll be sought after. You know how weird I am. I've never made friends easily."

"You made me."

"I'd hardly call that easy. I felt as if I was dragging you through a knothole."

"But it worked. And you knew how to do it. Don't worry, Mike. You'll have a lot more to choose from at UCLA than you've had here. And you'll still have me."

They each took a sip from their soft drinks.

"Mike—"

"Will—"

"You go first," Will said.

"No, you."

"Oh, okay. You'll know by this question just how far you've been able to get me through that knothole. I was wondering why we, I mean the two of us, after all, we're of opposite sexes, and yet, we've never, I mean, we've been friends without, well, you know. Don't you?"

She nodded. "That's just what I was wondering, and I couldn't have said it any better myself." Her legs were straight out in front of her and she stared at her dirty white sneakers. "Is it because you don't think I'm attractive?" she asked quietly. Then she raised her head and glared out the window at the far-off mountains. "Because if that's it, that's a stupid reason. The way people look has nothing to do with why you care about them. Or it shouldn't. If looks were everything, Cindy would be the most pop—"

"Cool down," Will said. "That's not it. You look fine."

"Just *fine?*"

"Oh, for Pete's sake. Okay, you look great. You look . . . unique. You look like you."

"Great, huh? Unique?" She smiled. "You look good to me, too. But you already know that."

"How would I know that? I'm just as insecure about my looks as you are. Maybe more."

"Yeah. I remember how you worried about your biceps. That's one thing I've never wasted any worry on."

"Let's not get competitive here. I'll bet you have other parts of your anatomy whose size you worry about and I don't."

"Which parts might you be referring to?" she asked indignantly.

"I'm only joking. To make a point. We both have insecurities—they're just about different things."

"But you're so cute and I'm so—oh, well, never mind. What about the original question? Have you really been thinking about that?"

"Sure. Haven't you? Here we are, at the peak of our hormonal vigor, both spending so much time with a member of the opposite species and behaving like monks."

"I think you got that part about the species right," Mike said. "And I know the answer. *My* answer, anyway. I need a friend. And I don't care what species it comes in. I need a friend more than I need anything else. And I'm not willing to risk losing a friendship by trying to make it into something more complicated." She gave him a sidelong look. "At least, not yet."

Will raised his eyebrows. "So you've thought about making it into something else?"

"Don't start preening your ego. Everybody thinks about stuff like that, if only fleetingly. Stop looking so pleased. It was *very* fleetingly."

"Of course. It was with me, too."

"Oh, so you had the same thought?"

He shrugged. "Just fleetingly. But I need a friend, too. And besides, I'm too socially inept and chicken to think about a *girl* friend."

"Oh, so a *girl* friend would get the benefit of a spiffed-up you, whereas I, as merely your friend, have to put up with an inept, chicken-livered jerk. Is that it?"

"I wouldn't have put it that way."

"I bet."

"But remember, you picked me. You knew we were going to be great friends. Was it the ineptness or the chicken-liverness that first attracted you?"

"Must have been the ineptness, a quality you've continued to refine."

He guffawed. "You know, I love this."

She giggled. "Me, too. There's nobody else I do this with."

"Me, neither."

"Just don't forget I'm female. Don't come around punching me in the arm and asking me to go with you to get tattooed."

He laughed. "No chance. If nothing else, those awful earrings will continue to remind me of your gender."

She laughed with him. "You've learned a lot from me, haven't you, big boy?"

As his laughter dwindled, he said, "That I have, Mike."

24

As the adobe neared completion, Will noticed they slowed their work, as if reluctant to finally have it done, putting an end to their almost daily association.

Since Will had responded to UCLA, the constraint among them was gone, and the last stages of building the house had been accomplished with a renewed pleasure in each other's company.

One afternoon early in May, they wandered through the rooms, looking for any last bits to finish off, and found none.

Mike got her camera and took long, loving footage of the warm, bright rooms, the carved lintels and vigas, the curved corner fireplaces, and for once she was silent. Sam leaned against the front doorframe, a root beer in his hand, and watched her. And Will, feeling strange and useless without a nail to hammer, a trench to dig, a boulder to push, watched them both.

Silence, broken only by the whirr of the camera, spread around them, out into the desert, enveloping them and the house they'd built into a living whole. When Mike shut off the camera, the stillness became absolute.

Will thought they might have stood there forever, had not a small lizard come curiously through the open front door and skittered across the cool tiles of the living-room floor, startling them all.

"I guess it's done," Sam said in a hoarse voice.

"I don't know how it could be more beautiful," Mike told him, her own voice tight.

After another long silence, Sam said, "You're lucky I didn't make you do the floors the way the old-timers did. They poured ox blood into the dirt and polished it. Took a nice, hard shine, too."

"When will you move the furniture in?" Will asked.

"Does that mean you don't want to help?" Sam said.

"I think you should do it yourself," Will said. "It's not our house anymore. It's yours." It made him sad to say that, but he didn't want Sam thinking he couldn't claim his own house now that it was done.

"It wouldn't be mine without the two of you," Sam said. "Your fingerprints are all over it as much as mine are."

"Surprise us," Mike said. "Get all moved in and then I'll come and take more pictures."

Will realized that they were conducting a ceremony, a rite of handing the house over to Sam, who would be staying, while he and Mike would leave. They would remember the house, but Sam would live in it.

He had the sense that they all knew what was happening, and he waited for Mike to put it into words, as she always did. When she didn't, he smiled and understood that she had learned from him, too.

25

By mid-May, Will swung between great apprehension and high elation. Two weeks to go. If Paige was going to cause trouble, wouldn't she have done it by now? Was he really going to make a clean getaway? Would he really be able to spend all summer conscience-free living and working near the beach, and go to UCLA with Mike in the fall? It looked as if he would.

Paige continued to meet with Truline in the afternoons and had recently begun going out every evening for what she called "spiritual experiences."

One evening, after an early supper, he set up the ironing board in Paige's phenomenally messy bedroom to press his graduation robe. He could hear her talking on the phone as he slid the iron back and forth, but he wasn't paying any attention. He was thinking about graduation and getting out of Agua Seca.

As he went to the closet in her room to look for a hanger, the air conditioner shut off and he clearly heard Paige say, "We might be able to leave before June 1."

He jerked his head out of the closet and listened tensely. Her voice was low, but the trailer was small and sound carried in a place as quiet as the desert.

"Well, as soon as we have the money, don't you think?

Unless we can raise more once we get to San Francisco."

San Francisco?

"Not yet, but I will. I have to pick the right time. He's sort of jumpy these days. Probably graduation, the excitement, you know. Okay. I'll see you in a while. Bye."

He came into the living room, unwittingly holding the hanger like a weapon in front of him.

"San Francisco?" he said.

She had the grace to look embarrassed, but not for long. "Yes. Such a sudden turn of events, but I know it's the right thing. A wonderful opportunity for growth."

"What are you talking about?" He still held the hanger menacingly before him.

"Come sit here, Will. And put that thing down. You look like Lizzie Borden. I need to talk to you."

Oh, no. Oh, no. Oh, no, he thought.

"The most wonderful thing is happening. Timothy and I are going to San Francisco. Together."

"I don't get it," he said, though he was sure he did. "I thought you were staying here for the summer. I thought Timothy wanted space." Suddenly, her evenings spent on spiritual experience made sense. Timothy was the experience.

"Well, now he wants me in it with him. We're going to open a vegetarian restaurant. My experience here will be invaluable. So will yours."

"A vegetarian restaurant?" He felt explosive. "What happened to animal rights?"

"Can you think of a better way to protect animals than to discourage killing them for food?"

"Do you have any idea how much it costs to open a restaurant?" He jumped to his feet and paced the tiny living room, waving the hanger. "Do you have any idea how many vegetarian restaurants there must be already in San Francisco?"

"Calm down. We know what we're doing. You're right about the money, though. We'll need some investors. I wondered if you'd be interested."

"Me?" He stopped pacing. "I haven't got any money."

"UCLA's giving you lots of money. You probably don't have to use it right away. You and Timothy and I could start the restaurant with it and you can go to UCLA later, after we're established."

"Are you crazy? That would be fraud. If I went with you, which I'm not going to do, I'd have to sacrifice that money. And UCLA. What about Truline and all the peaceful serenity here?"

"It'll be here, waiting for me, if I need it. And I'll take what I've learned from Truline with me. She taught me how to pray and it worked. What I asked for was given to me, what I sought I found. I knocked and it was opened to me."

"I don't think you've learned anything." He crashed back onto the couch. "Truline must be outraged."

"No, she's not. She says it's important to spread the Good News. *She's* giving us some money for our restaurant."

He turned away. "It's true. Everybody here is mentally impaired."

She touched his arm. "You know Sam Webb a lot better than I do. Would you ask him if he'd like to be an investor?"

"I'd cut out my tongue first."

"Will, what's wrong? You've always supported me before. Sometimes reluctantly, but you've always come around. This is such an exciting idea. You have to come with us. We don't want to go without you. We're counting on you to be the cook."

He'd done such a fine job of convincing himself that everything was going to work out this time, he was actually surprised by her insistence. He didn't use to get surprised, when his defenses were always up.

He saw himself getting older and more bitter, following Paige and whomever she was with at the time, from calamity to calamity, explaining and mending and paying for their heedlessness.

He turned to face her. "No, I don't want to go. I'm going to UCLA, and you and Timothy can go wherever you want. You can get into any kind of fix you want and you can bail yourselves out. Or not, whatever you want. That'll be your life. I'm having a different one."

"Oh, come on, Will. Don't be difficult. We need you. Besides, it'll be fun. An adventure."

"Paige. Do you ever hear anything I say? Watch my lips. I'm going to UCLA."

"We'll talk about this later," she said, taking up her purse and digging out her car keys. "I have to meet Timothy to do some planning."

"There's not enough planning in the whole world to keep you and Timothy out of trouble."

"I wish you could hear how silly you sound. You can't believe that. See you later, sweetie."

As soon as the door closed behind her, Will picked a pillow off the sofa and punched it viciously twice before he threw it onto the floor.

"I'm going to UCLA," he said aloud. "I mean it. I

don't care how stupid Paige's plan is. I don't care how sure I am that she'll need help in a couple of months. I don't care how pitiful and needy she'll be when she asks me for something. I can't stand any more of this. I won't give in."

Was he going to be able to convince himself, he wondered. He'd never been able to make himself immune to Paige's need. He always felt it, and his answering need to fix things for her, to set her on her feet one more time. He felt the terrible urgent pull of obligation.

He heard a car engine shut off outside. Of course she's forgotten something. She couldn't even leave the house with herself organized. How does she imagine she could run a business?

He jerked open the front door and saw Mike, her hand raised to knock.

"Don't shoot," she said. "What's the matter?"

"I thought you were Paige." He shut the door behind her.

"I guess she told you about the vegetarian-restaurant plan, then."

"How do you know about that?"

"That's why I came over. Marcella just got a call from Timothy asking for money. Excuse me, I mean *investors*."

"He asked your mother? What did she say?"

"No, of course. She only met him once, when she was looking for somebody to do one day's worth of heavy labor at the dig. He declined because he was afraid he'd hurt his fine musician's hands. Have you ever seen him play any kind of instrument?"

Will stamped around the living room. "I should have

known she'd tell me last. She just assumed I'd go along with the idea."

"Will you?"

He hesitated, then said, "Get serious. Anybody can see what a harebrained scheme it is. Anybody but Paige and Timothy."

"That's a relief. I was afraid I'd find you writing to UCLA telling them you'd decided to go into the restaurant business."

"Is that why you really came over? To check up on me?"

"Don't displace your anger at Paige onto me. Save it until she gets home."

"Displace my anger? Where do you get this stuff? Can't I be angry at you *and* Paige at the same time?"

"Except that I haven't done anything to make you angry and Paige has."

"Who says you haven't done anything to make me angry? What about assuming I'd give up all my plans to accommodate Paige?"

"Tell the truth. Weren't you thinking about it?"

He stalked into the kitchenette and opened the refrigerator. Sometimes he thought she was gifted with second sight. He took out a root beer. He kept root beer in the refrigerator and he couldn't stand the stuff.

He went back into the living room and handed the unopened can to Mike.

"What's this?" she asked.

"It's a root beer. Are you blind?"

She smiled. "Peace offering accepted."

"It's not a peace offering. It's a root beer."

"That shows how much you know." She dropped the can into her big black bag. "Why don't we get out of here. Away from the scene of the crime."

"What did you have in mind?"

"We can go to the Prickly Pear and listen to music. Or we can go admire Sam's house. Or take a walk in the desert."

"Let's go see Sam. I haven't seen him much since the house was finished. I thought he'd like to be alone with it for a while." With Sam and Mike, maybe he would feel safe from his own foolish, irresistible impulses.

"What a quaint idea. Sort of like newlyweds."

Will laughed. "Sort of. Let's go."

26

The lights were on at Sam's and the house looked beautiful, glowing and bonded into the earth. Will could hardly think what this place must have looked like before the house appeared. It seemed to belong in just this spot.

Sam opened the door. "Hello, strangers. I was starting to think you only loved me for my construction site."

"Will thought we should leave you and the house alone for a while, to get acquainted. They say the first year together is the hardest."

"This house and I were friends when it was just a sketch on the back of an envelope. We can stand to have a couple of pals over. Come on in."

"It looks like you've lived here forever," Will said. Even the furniture from the trailer looked different, surrounded by the warm beige walls. Will remembered the plastering of those walls, the arduous process of applying the brown coat, then the finish coat, and finally the smooth coat of Keene's cement plaster, but he'd never thought, while he was working with sweat in his eyes, that what he'd done would look so fine by lamplight. Overhead, the yellow-chalk-marked viga seemed a work of art.

"I wish I had," Sam said. "Sit down. You want a beer?"

"A Coke'll be fine. Mike's brought her own."

Mike pulled the can from her bag and took it to the kitchen. Will followed them and took down glasses as Sam found ice and Mike popped the cans.

"What's this I hear about Paige and Timothy?" Sam asked. "Last time I looked, they weren't speaking. Now I understand they're going into business."

Will groaned. "How come everybody else knew about this before me? I thought Timothy was safely out of the picture, all taken up by Cindy—"

Mike snorted.

"—and that Paige had found the way, the truth, and the light with Truline."

Mike snorted again.

"Paige and Timothy," Sam said. "They're two of a kind. I heard about their scheme when Truline told me this morning she was investing in their restaurant. She thinks the sun rises and sets on those two."

"Then she's as crazy as they are," Will said.

"Could be," Sam said.

"They even wanted to use my scholarship money."

"You didn't tell me that," Mike exclaimed. "What a lot of nerve, even if such a thing was legal."

Will felt no rush of words in Paige's defense, the way he usually did when she was being criticized. It *had* been a lot of nerve. How could he defend that?

"They want you to go with them?" Sam asked.

"How did you know?"

Sam shrugged. "Lucky guess. You going?"

"Why are you and Mike so convinced I'll be tempted to go with them? Don't you give me any credit for having a mind of my own?"

Neither Mike nor Sam said a word.

"Whoa," Will said. "You still think Paige can jerk me around any time she wants?"

"How did you happen to get to Agua Seca in the first place?" Mike asked. "Why weren't you going to college? Why—"

"The college thing was mostly money," Will interrupted.

"Right. Why are you even thinking about something as crazy as going to San Francisco with Paige and Timothy? Why—"

"Who says I am?" he interrupted again.

Mike just gave him a knowing look. "Why did you always clean up after Paige at the Snakebite even when it was her turn?"

Will spread his hands. "I'm just a good guy."

"Well, you better quit being such a good guy. It gets you nothing but trouble with Paige."

"Okay, okay. Can we talk about something else now if you're through assassinating my character?"

"I'm just trying to—" Mike started.

"That's enough, Mike," Sam cut in. "Will knows."

He locked his bedroom door when he got home, and opened his window all the way to relieve the claustrophobic atmosphere in the tiny room. It would be just like Paige to want to come in and wake him up to talk, the way she did when she was high with anticipation of some new escapade.

He lay with his hands behind his head, wide awake. He understood what Mike and Sam were telling him. But they didn't understand how it was with him and Paige; how they were family, how they needed to be together, how he'd promised his mother he'd look out for her. All of that counted, too. Maybe more than satisfying his own selfish desire to be at UCLA. He'd been thinking of studying art, improving his carving, but he could do that anywhere. San Francisco was supposed to be hospitable to artists.

He heard Paige's car, the fan belt still whining, drive up and stop. He heard her key in the lock, her footsteps in the hall, the small rattle of his doorknob as she tested it. There was a silence and then she rattled the knob again, a little louder, while he hoped she wouldn't knock. He didn't want to talk to her now. He was too susceptible to her when she was breathless and bursting with a new plan. He was already too afraid he was going to go with her.

He fell asleep and dreamed of a restaurant in San Francisco, a place he'd never been, where Paige worked with flowers in her hair, where Timothy played the guitar for the diners, and where he, Will, cooked, and where he sold his carved animals in a case by the cash register. Every one of the carved animals was a black dog.

27

Will carried another suitcase to Paige's car and wedged it into the trunk. "I can't get any more in here," he told her. "The rest'll have to go in the back seat."

"Okay," she called from inside the trailer. "There's not too much more. Just my bag of shoes and the cooler."

Timothy had been sitting in the passenger seat for half an hour, waiting for Paige to finish packing, his feet in a pile of fashion magazines and empty Diet Coke cans. "I don't know, man," Timothy said to Will. "How come women need so much stuff? It's best to make the journey lightly."

Will shrugged. "Nesting instinct? It's misplaced on Paige."

Finally Paige came out of the trailer. She wore shorts and new pink tennis shoes. She'd changed her hair color to a purplish red and permed it into an electric frizz around her face. Will couldn't get used to it. She was jittery and excited and hadn't been able to sleep for three nights. He'd heard her roaming around the trailer, opening cupboards and flipping the TV off and on while he, too, lay awake.

She bounced into the driver's seat, reached over to grab

Timothy around the neck and give him a kiss, and turned on the ignition without closing her door.

"Come on, Will. Get in. It's not too late."

He stood, holding her door, smiling and shaking his head. "Yeah, it is. This is your life now. Have a good one." He bent into the open door and kissed his sister's cheek. "Write to me and let me know your address."

"Once we're a success, you'll be sorry you didn't come."

"A chance I'll have to take." He shut the door and leaned on the open window frame. She'd never gotten the air-conditioning fixed. "Bye, you two."

"Take it gently," Timothy said, as Paige put the car into reverse.

"Bye, little brother. I'm telling you, you'll be sorry."

Will stood and waved as the car backed around the corner of the Snakebite, straightened, and entered the highway. Paige blew the horn several times, and waved out the open window until he couldn't see her anymore.

He went back in to the cool, dim shambles of the trailer, where he spent the morning cleaning Paige's bedroom. Then he cleaned himself up. Mike was taking him out to Sam's for lunch.

They'd been treating him kindly and tenderly like someone recovering from a long illness, and maybe that's what he was doing. He had some of the same feelings of unsteadiness and fear of relapse that he got after a bout of the flu.

It was strange to think he didn't know when he'd see Paige again, and to know that he'd see her only if he chose to. The kind of grief he felt was different, he knew, from the grief Sam felt for his son, or from that he felt for his mother, but it was a grief of loss, all the same.

The next morning he'd be taking the bus back to Imperial Beach, where Chuck had agreed to let him use his old bedroom for the summer. Chuck liked the house and wanted to stay, and Will could use the income. He would save Paige's portion until he knew where to send it, and it would be hers to waste as she saw fit.

Then, at the end of the summer, Mike would come for him from Nova Scotia, Marcella's next stop, and they'd drive to UCLA together.

A whole summer by the beach again: his anticipation was so acute it almost hurt. He could hardly remember what it was like to sleep all night with the sounds of surf in his ears, to wake up to the aqueous light on the ceiling of his room that came straight from reflection off the water, to be able to pull on a pair of shorts and walk along the tide line, ankle-deep in sea-foam, before breakfast, breathing in the moist, salty air. All his senses were thirsty for the ocean.

He stood in the doorway of Paige's tidy room, the surest symbol that she was really gone. It had never looked like this when she'd lived there. He raised his eyes and looked out her window into a landscape drowned in glaring light, one he'd come to respect and understand. The way he had himself.

"I thought you'd better have one last bowl of my potent chili before you go back to civilization and have to settle for whatever poor stuff you can find there," Sam said, filling bowls for lunch. "At least you'll remember me until the scars heal."

"I'll remember you a lot longer than that," Will said, pouring root beer for Sam and Mike.

Sam made a rough sound in his throat and carried two bowls to the table. Will brought the other bowl and his Coke. Mike sat at the table, her chin propped on her palm, waiting for them. When they were all three seated, Mike said, "Is that it? Is that all you two are going to say to each other about leaving?"

"Come on, Mike," Will said. "We're just simple men, the way you keep reminding us. We can't manage one of those emotional scenes that comes so easily to you. We know what we mean."

She dipped her spoon into the chili. "I guess you do. I like to have real words in my mind to remember, not just suggestions of perhaps an emotion."

"Well, that's all you're going to get from us," Sam said, "so lay off. I think we've been very patient, putting up with your excessive need for emotional expression. Just once, let us be strong and silent."

"Oh, all right. I think this chili is a plot to destroy my vocal apparatus, anyway," she wheezed.

On the coffee table stood a carving of a black dog romping in the surf. Will knew it was the best thing he'd ever made. He'd stained it and polished it with care, knowing it would be Sam's, and he wanted it to last forever.

The chili was a good excuse for the tears in all their eyes.